DAYS OF WRATH

BY ANDRÉ MALRAUX

DAYS OF WRATH (LE TEMPS DU MÉPRIS)

THE ROYAL WAY (LA VOIE ROYALE)

MAN'S FATE (LA CONDITION HUMAINE)

Days of Wrath

BY ANDRÉ MALRAUX

TRANSLATED BY HAAKON M. CHEVALIER

MCMXXXVI

RANDOM HOUSE · NEW YORK CITY

TO THE GERMAN COMRADES

Who were anxious for me to
make known what they had suffered and what they had upheld,

THIS BOOK, WHICH IS THEIRS

Author's Preface

The articles devoted to this short novel at the time of its serial publication suggest a number of ideas to which I wish to call attention very briefly, and which I hope to develop more fully on a future occasion.

Those who believe my documentation to have been too sketchy are referred to the *official* regulations governing the concentration camps. I do not define the National-Socialist party by its concentration camps; what we know of French prisons allows no complacency on that score. But it is the concentration camps that are dealt with here.

The world of a work like this, the world of tragedy, is the ancient world still—man, the crowd, the elements, woman, destiny. It reduces itself to two characters, the hero and his sense of life; individual antagonisms, which make possible the complexity of the full length novel, do not figure here. If I had had to give Nazis the importance which I give Kassner, I should obviously have done so in terms of their basic emotional drive—nationalism.

The illustrious example of Flaubert is perhaps more misleading than any other. Flaubert (for whom the value of art was supreme, and who, indeed, placed the artist above the saint and the hero) created only characters whom he was able to regard with complete emotional detachment. He could even go so far as to write: "I shall make them all wallow in the same mud—to be perfectly fair." Such an attitude would have been utterly incomprehensible to Aeschylus or Corneille, to Hugo or Chateaubriand, or even Dostoyevsky. Yet it would have been approved—as indeed it is—by many authors with whom it would be futile to contrast them. Two essential notions of art are here involved. Nietzsche regarded Wagner as a mountebank insofar as he subordinated his genius to his characters. But one may wish the word Art to mean an attempt

4

to give men a consciousness of their own hidden greatness.

It is not emotion that destroys a work of art, but the desire to demonstrate something; the value of such a work depends neither upon its emotion nor its detachment, but upon the blending of its content with the method of its expression. And if the work's value, justification, and chances of lasting reside in its *quality*, its content—regardless of the author's intention—alters the existing emotional scale; without an inexorable necessity for such alteration the work would doubtless not have come into being. The history of artistic sensibility in France for the past fifty years might be called the death-agony of the brotherhood of man. Its real enemy is an unformulated individualism which existed sporadically throughout the nineteenth century and which sprang less from the will to create a man whole than from a fanatical desire to be different. Artistic individualism is concerned above all in safeguarding the "inner world," and is justified only when it is applied to the domain of feeling or of dreams; for in the realm of action, to take a concrete example, the "giants" of the Renaissance were always obliged to transform themselves into relic-bearing donkeys, and the figure of Cæsar Borgia loses its radiance if one considers that his greatest effectiveness was due to the prestige of the Church. Contempt for men is common among politicians, but not avowed. It was not only in Stendhal's time that concrete conditions of social life imposed hypocrisy on the pure individualist whenever he wished to act.

The individual stands in opposition to society, but he is nourished by it. And it is far less important to know what differentiates him than what nourishes him. Like the genius, the individual is valuable for what there is within him. To refer again to the past, the Christian had as true an existence as the modern individual, and a soul is just as

6

valuable as a differentiation. Every psychological life is an exchange, and the fundamental problem of the living individual is knowing upon what he intends to feed.

In Kassner's opinion as in that of some other communist intellectuals, communism restores to the individual all the creative potentialities of his nature. If he happens to be a subject of the Roman Empire, an early Christian, a soldier of the French revolution, a Soviet worker, a man is an integral part of the society in which he lives; if, on the other hand, he is an Alexandrian or an eighteenth century French writer, he is separate from it, and, unless he identifies himself with the social order which is struggling to be born, his essential expression cannot be heroic. There are of course other human attitudes. . . .

It is difficult to be a man. But it is not more difficult to become one by enriching one's fellowship with other men than by cultivating one's individual peculiarities. The former nourishes with at least as much force as the latter that which makes man human, which enables him to surpass himself, to create, invent or realize himself.

ANDRÉ MALRAUX

Chapter One

At the moment when Kassner was pushed into the guard room, a prisoner under cross-examination finished a sentence which was drowned in the shuffle of papers and police boots. Across the table from him sat the Hitler official. He was true to type: heavy jaws, square head, close cropped blond hair, almost shaved over the ears.

". . . instructions of the party."

"Since when?"

"1924."

"What were your official functions in the underground communist party?"

"I'm not familiar with the underground party. Until January, 1933, my functions in the German party were of a purely technical nature."

The communist shifted his position, almost turning his back to Kassner. The voices and the faces no longer matched. The prisoner's voice was rather low and impersonal, as though he meant to convey by its very tone that it was not *he* who was answering, but some irresponsible person under compulsion. The voice of the official was casual, even more youthful than his youthful profile. Kassner waited for this adolescent, upon whom his own case depended, to reveal himself by voice and words.

The latter looked at the prisoner, who was merely staring into space.

"You have been to Russia."

"Yes, as a technician: I was attached to the Electrozavod."

"We'll look into that. What was your function in the German republic of the Volga?"

"Never seen it. Nor the Volga."

"What cell did you belong to in Berlin?"

"Ex-1015."

"We'll look into that. Under whose direction?"

The communist's back was now completely turned, and Kassner listened for the answer.

"A man named Hans."

"I could have told you that myself. What I want to know is his last name. Don't try to make a fool of me, you son of a bitch."

"We only know our comrades by their first names. That's a strict rule."

"What about his address?"

"I've never seen him outside the cell."

"All right! I'm going to put you in one of our cells. You'll be surprised how that will refresh your memory. How long were you in Moabit?"

"Six months."

"Hundred and eighty days since your arrest? . . ."

Kassner only now began to think of his own. The SA-men[1] had taken him in a bus for the first stage of the journey. (With its Nazi pas-

[1] Sturmabteilung—Storm Troopers, who wear brown shirts.

sengers, it had been more oppressively close than a police truck.) Among his several activities, he was in charge of a small factory manufacturing variable pitch propellers, and was entitled to the use of an airplane on occasion: there the plane was resting, in its hangar, and during the whole journey Kassner had been able to think of nothing else. At a street-corner they had passed some painters who sang while they repainted a chandler's shop-front, as many-coloured as the Red Square. . . . Until now all that had seemed unreal to him, but more like a ritual than a dream.

"Hundred and eighty . . ." resumed the official. "Well, well. . . . By the way, who's sleeping with your wife all this time?"

Did the prisoner, whom the official fixed with his gaze, acknowledge the hit? Kassner felt him intensely present, at once riveted to the spot with his whole helplessness, and absent with his whole strength. The official's tone was no longer aggressive.

"Who sleeps with your wife?" he repeated.

Kassner began to put himself in the communist's place; it was confusing to be both spectator and suffering actor.

"I am not married," answered the prisoner, whose profile again became visible.

Another silence.

"That doesn't prevent you from having a woman . . ." said the Nazi at last with the same indifferent voice.

The two men looked at each other now with a tired disgust.

The official made a motion with his chin: two SA-men led the prisoner away, then pushed Kassner towards the table. The Nazi looked at him, opened a record-file and took out a photograph.

Like all those who sometimes have occasion to hide their identity, Kassner was thoroughly familiar with his own long equine face, its firm-set jaws. What picture was the Hitler official examining? Kassner saw it upside down. Not very dangerous: at that time his head was shaved, and the expression in the narrow, bony face, with its pointed ears, was appreciably different from the one he revealed at present, beneath his longish crop of chestnut hair—the look of a broken-down thoroughbred, vaguely romantic. In the photograph his lips were tightly closed; he knew that when he smiled his long teeth showed to the gums. Biting his lower lip likewise exposed his teeth. He did so—just slightly, for he had an aching molar—and lowered his glance to the table: his large eyes had a way of looking slightly upward at an object, and by merely seeming to lower them he could blot out the white slit between the iris and the lower lid.

Without saying a word, the Nazi alternately scrutinized the picture and the face. Kassner knew that if he was recognized he would be killed—with or without trial.

"Kassner," said the Nazi.

All the scribblers or SA-men raised their heads.

And for the first time Kassner saw his record written on hostile faces.

"I am known in my legation. The most idiotic conspirator does not ask members of the police militia for a light and walk into a trap under their very eyes."

The scene of his arrest came back to him in all its vividness. He was with several comrades in a little antique shop kept by one of them, half an hour before a dental appointment, when one of the members of the illegal organization had come in, hung his coat over a pile of dalmatics, ikons, chasubles, and other orthodox ornaments, and said as he sat down: "The police have set a trap at Wolf's. They're going to raid the place."

Wolf had got up.

"I have a list of names in my watch-case. . . ."

They had instructions never to leave names on their premises.

"You'll be arrested as you go in. Where is your watch?"

"In the closet, in the pocket of the black vest. But it's . . ."

"No nonsense: the list! Give me the keys."

On arriving, Kassner had met two SA-men in the hall. It was no longer even a trap. He stopped in front of them, tried to light the cigarette between his lips with an empty lighter, asked the SA-men for a light, went upstairs. In ringing the bell, he leaned against the door to hide his hand as he inserted the key, entered, shut the door, opened the closet, took the watch, put the list in his mouth, replaced the watch and reshut the closet door. No footsteps on the stairs. He would be arrested when he went down. Nowhere in this room to throw the door-key, and to open the window would have been absurd. He slipped it into the pocket of one of the trousers hanging in the closet: Wolf might have several keys.

He would wait five minutes, as if he had come to pay Wolf a visit and had not found him in. The taste of the paper he was chewing with consider-

able pain (was it neuralgia or his bad tooth? If only
this had happened after the dentist!) reminded him
of the pasteboard smell of carnival masks. At best, it
would not be easy to get out of this. False identifi-
cation papers cannot be counted on for much. . . .
And he did not look forward to the Nazi prisons
with any optimism. Who knows the limits of his
own endurance? How many times had he been told
that prisoners on hard labor wear themselves out
to obtain a little extra food, so that when they are
released they are unfit for their illegal organization work. He threw away his cigarette: added
to the taste of the chewed paper, that of tobacco
was nauseating him. Then he had gone out, and had
been arrested on the landing.

"At my factory you will find a correspondence
of more than fifteen letters between Mr. Wolf and
ourselves, don't you see," said Kassner. "All the
goods have been delivered."

19

The illegal organization had taken precautions. The Pilsen accent was not bad, but Kassner was really from Munich. He had formed the habit, when he was doing party work, of casually slipping the phrase "don't you see," into his speech; it revolted him to speak cordially to Nazis; he watched himself—to no avail—and spoke slowly. Both men knew how difficult it is to prove the spuriousness of a minutely prepared false identity. The Nazi skimmed through the record, raised his eyes, again examined the record.

A photograph, Kassner was thinking, and the description—what else? What about all those sheets? The SA had verified the fact that Kassner had asked him for a light. But how had he entered? The key had not been found on him, granted, and they had heard him ring; but would they believe that the door had been unlocked? . . .

How did his life look on those bits of paper? A miner's son; a scholarship student at the University, the organizer of one of the proletarian theaters; a prisoner in Russia who had gone over to the party, and then to the Red Army; a delegate to China and Mongolia; a writer, returned to Germany to prepare the Ruhr strikes against the Papen decree, an organizer of the illegal intelligence service, a former vice-president of the Red Aid. . . . Enough evidence to have him shot, obviously, but quite compatible with a happy-go-lucky character.

"It's not any more difficult to go to the legation with false papers than into the street," said the Nazi.

But Kassner felt him hesitate. And all those about him were hesitating. People instinctively feel that a romantic life should betray itself in a picturesque face. It seemed as though Kassner, the chronicler of the Siberian civil war, whose accounts of his experiences were so intensely vivid and revealed such a robust gift for communicating powerful emotions, was expected to carry with him the dramas which he had lived and described, and his life became confused with the epic of rag-clad Siberia. Moreover,

21

his presence in Germany since Hitler's triumph was known, and all the defeated treasured in him both the companion (his rôle was an important, but not a crucial one) and the future chronicler of their oppression. Even for his enemies his person was identified with what he had experienced, like a traveler with the country he has traveled through, like a bystander with the catastrophe he has narrowly escaped. All expected a face which bore traces of Siberia; no doubt they had found such traces in the photographs published in the newspapers not so long ago, where it was easy to supply them. A living face lent itself less easily to such modifications. Almost all those who hesitated were ready to ridicule the idea that this fellow might be Kassner. The official left the room, returned, closed his file, and made the same motion with his chin as at the end of the preceding examination. Two SA-men pushed Kassner towards the door, then with a series of blows and kicks (nothing, however, beyond the conventional military brutality) towards the prison.

If they had decided to finish me right away, thought Kassner, they would have led me to the guard house.

But no: corridors, and more corridors.

He was finally incarcerated in a rather large dark hole.

After some minutes, the darkness was gradually absorbed by the walls, whose gray paint began to appear. Kassner paced round the cell, idly active, thinking without being conscious of his thoughts; he became aware of this, and stopped walking. It struck him that the wall was dirtiest by the door, and close to the floor. Because of those who, like himself had walked there? But there was no dust. The cell had a German cleanliness; hygienic. . . . Was it dampness? Already he perceived that his questions were mechanical: while his mind went round in a circle, like his idiotic body (I must look more and more like a horse), his eyes had ceased roving, they had understood quicker than his brain: the wall, at its base, was covered with writing.

In order to escape from the present, his thoughts grasped at everything that came within their reach. But what could he think about? If he was identified, it was merely a question of whether they would soon come to kill him, to torture him, or merely to beat him into unconsciousness; he might as well read the inscriptions on the walls.

Many were partly rubbed out. Some were written in code. (If I have to stay here, I'll try to decipher them.) Others were quite clear. He resumed pacing round the cell, very slowly, focussed his eyes on the most legible ones, and read, as he drew nearer: "I don't want . . ." The rest, rubbed out. Another: "Dying in the street would have been less rotten, after all, than to die here." Several times, since becoming a prisoner, Kassner had told himself that if they had used actual violence they might have won over that majority of workers which they needed; but he was keenly aware of the romantic streak in his own make-up, and was on his guard against it. A phrase of Lenin's obsessed him: "You cannot win with the vanguard alone." Since his return to Germany, Kassner had felt that it was impossible to create unity among the workers without activity in the reformist and Catholic trade unions, that the work within the trade unions and the factories was insufficient to train them adequately for militant struggle: the revolutionary workers were the first to be laid off; they had been forced into the handicrafts, and barely one tenth of the party was active in the great factories. The year before, there had been fewer strikes in Germany than in France, England, the United States. . . . Kassner had been active in organizing the red trade unions: their membership had grown to more than three hundred thousand by the end of the year. But this was still too little.

25

Now, with Hitler in power, it was necessary to organize the union of all the revolutionary forces within the factories themselves and to unite these forces on issues raised by the day-to-day developments, which must be transmitted as quickly as possible and effectively linked with the activities initiated by the base-organizations. Kassner had accordingly been working since January in the intelligence service; it was one of the most dangerous, and the most legible inscriptions—the most recent—had no doubt almost all been written by men belonging to it. He drew close to another one: "My hair is still black"; and as if the choice of this inscription had originated in some sharper, surer force within him than his sight, footsteps became audible.

The sounds became jumbled: three, four men; five at least, perhaps six.

Six SA-men could be coming here—together—at this hour, only to use violence.

The door of a distant cell opened, and closed

again on the clatter of boots which suddenly sank into the wool of silence.

The thing to be feared was not so much suffering or death; it was the sadistic ingenuity of those on whom the door had just closed. Throughout the world, it is always the most degraded who choose this calling. And the tormentor is always stronger than his victim in the last stages of humiliation or suffering.

"If they were to torture me to make me give information which I didn't have, I could do nothing about it. So let's assume I don't know anything."

His courage at this moment was intent upon separating the man who in a few minutes would be in the power of that menacing shuffle of boots from the Kassner he would once more become.

The power of the prison was such that even the guards spoke almost in a whisper. A scream sud-

27

denly filled his cell, drawn out to the limit of the breath, and finally smothered in a gasp.

He must seek refuge in complete passivity, in the irresponsibility of sleep and madness; and yet keep watch with a mind sufficiently lucid to be able to defend himself, not to let himself be destroyed here irremediably; tear himself asunder so as to yield only what was unessential.

The cry rang out again. Sharper, this time. Kassner pressed his fingers into his ears. But it was useless: his mind had already seized the rhythm of the pain from which those shrieks were torn, and awaited the cry at the very moment it was repeated. He had been through the war, but he had never heard the screams of a tortured man within closed walls. The war-wounded moaned, and their cries had nothing in common with these, especially terrifying because of their mystery. In what way were they torturing this man who was yelling, how would he himself soon be tortured? Torture in the open air suddenly seemed a boon.

28

The door closed, and the steps came towards his cell.

He realized that he was leaning against the wall of his cell as if his back were glued to it, with his shoulders hunched. He was firm, but his knees were not. He left the wall, exasperated by the limpness of his legs.

A second door slammed shut on the footsteps, as if it had captured them in passing. Silence over a seething nest of tiny sounds.

He turned again towards the door: "*Stahl was killed the . . .*" The sentence was unfinished this time, not obliterated; the wall exuded human destinies.

He remembered a letter from a prisoner's wife: "How they beat him! I couldn't recognize him, Therese, among the others. . . ."

How many of his comrades would come here after him? His pencil had not yet been taken from him. *We are with you*, he wrote.

On removing his hand, he read another inscription: *Before a month is up I am going to kill Feder-wisch.* This was the man who had been but lately one of the camp wardens. Which one was dead, the threatener or the man who was threatened?

Even as his roaming eyes seized the scrawled lines, his alert ears caught the sounds of the guards' foot-steps, vague scratchings in the neighboring cells, and a sudden outburst of abuse in some outer court, at once choked by the corridors and clarified by distance. . . . Still no cry. He was beginning to live entirely in a world of hostile sounds and noises, like a menaced blind man.

He knew how difficult it is to submit to blows without retaliating. And he fully realized where his strength lay—the whole-hearted self-surrender which often enabled him to penetrate to that be-numbed region of a man's heart in which the mem-ory of his dead is still vivid; but he was not eager to talk to the Nazis. Besides, it was not the disinter-ested followers of Hitler who had chosen to be prison-guards; Kassner knew moreover that if every man is capable of killing in the heat of combat, it requires surrender to an abject loyalty to strike a prisoner. All he had to do was to say nothing. He did not have to answer blows by memorable words, he had to get away in order to resume his revolutionary work. And perhaps he would be beaten to death; but he remembered that at Hagen, in a factory of seven hundred and fifty workers, it had been impossible in spite of the terror to discover a single one of those who had distributed leaflets.

"You'll see how that will improve your memory. . . ."

He remained standing in the middle of the cell, his elbows tightly pressing against his ribs, still waiting for another cry. Nothing. And yet, as the cell which the SA-men had just entered was closer than the one before, he thought he heard deadened blows. . . . Then, while he was still on the alert for a cry, there came a choked yelp, more distinct between the two metallic sounds of the opening and closing of a door.

31

The steps again—very close this time. Kassner walked to the door of his cell, which opened the moment he reached it.

Four SA-men entered, two remained in the corridor. Heads were lowered and arms menacingly advanced—lighted only by a storm-lantern which one of them had put down on the floor.

These were not the tragic figures he had imagined. In their postures—arms sticking out from the shoulders, crooked at the elbows, like Hercules and the chimpanzees—they were caricatures of brutality. His terror vanished. It had been a primitive terror, a fear of suffering united with the unknown; and perhaps he had particularly expected the sadist, the drunkard, the madman—the inhuman. These men were not drunk. What about sadism? But now that they were present, exaltation and firmness had replaced terror.

They were watching him. And no doubt they could see him no better than he saw them—formless, with only the chin and cheeks lighted from below, and surmounted by their heavy shadows which sprang to the ceiling like enormous spiders. For the second time he felt himself squeezed into a cavity in the earth, with all the rock of the prison piled around it. The light struck his own cheeks, too, from below; painfully; but no, it was his jaws, which he was clenching with all his might, that caused the pain. He noticed, bitterly, that he no longer suffered from his aching tooth. He resolved not to draw back a step.

The blow of a fist in the stomach doubled him over as though he had suddenly caved in; and the moment his face dropped, another blow to the chin threw him violently backward; his ribs met simultaneously the hard resistance of the cement floor and the boots which began to kick at him. The mildness of the pain astonished him, though its violence was such that he was at the very edge of consciousness; with torture close at hand, and all that he had imagined, there was something ridiculous about being beaten like this. As he had rolled

33

over on his belly, the soft parts of his body were protected. Beneath the blows, his belly seemed the center of a protective cage of ribs and bones on which the boots were savagely hammering. A kick in the jaw: he felt himself spitting blood, and when he heard: "What, you're spitting your own flag?" a red blotch flashed and crackled before his eyes— it was from a kick in the nape of the neck. Then he fainted.

He had a confused sense of being flung into another cell, with the cry: "Auf wiedersehen!"

When the door of his cell again closed, his first sensation was one of comfort. This door whose crushing weight hung over him protected him from the abjectness and the absurdity outside; and at the same time the solitude, the bareness, and the end of unconsciousness brought him back that dim sense of being enclosed which he had experienced in childhood, when he played Indian under the tables. He felt only relief.

34

Would the night soon end? A guard opened a peep-hole in the door for an instant and then shut it: by the light from the corridor Kassner saw on the back wall of his cell a grill which seemed to protect a ventilation hole, narrow and deep like a machicolation. As this hole had been walled in, it did not connect his cell with the outer world, it lived a self-sufficient and stifled life; it alone made sentient the crushing thickness of the stone. Kassner was in a vault, separated from the world as by sleep, by madness; but the hole gave the life-like quality of a creature's shell to the thick suffocating stone, which was riddled with cells where those prisoners who could still walk moved about like tireless centipedes.

He sought the wall, struck it with his bent forefinger. Several knocks at long intervals. No answer.

The exaltation had vanished with the struggle. The sense of well-being which had benumbed Kassner when the door had shut was rotting into anguish: it was slipping away in shreds, from his sensitive skin, from his clothes which had become limp like night-garments; with his suspenders and shoe-laces torn away, the buttons cut off (he was not to commit suicide), the substance of the cloth seemed to have changed. What was it that was crushing him? The hole in the wall? Or was it the pain gradually piercing through his fever? Or the night? Convicts who are incarcerated in round cells, where there is nothing for the eye to fasten on, always go mad.

He knocked again.

The two threads of light at right angles which still outlined the door disappeared.

His strength, grown parasitic, was gnawing him relentlessly. He was an animal of action, and the darkness was draining his will-power.

He must wait. That was all. Hold out. Live in a state of suspended animation, like the paralyzed, like the dying, with the same submerged tenacity— like a face in the very heart of darkness.

Otherwise, madness.

Chapter Two

How many days?

Complete darkness, except for the rounds, and an occasional ray of light between the door and the jamb. How many days alone with madness, as pervasively present as a toad's feeble croaking?

The beatings in the neighboring cells continued.

Outside it was perhaps daylight. A real daylight full of trees and grass and zinc roofs bluish in the morning light.

Although his wife was in Prague, during the last twenty minutes he had felt certain that she was dead. Dead, while he was here, caged like an animal. He could see her face, with its vague resemblance to a mulatto's, serene as are the faces of the dead, her too full lips slightly drawn, her waved hair straggling, her eyelids lowered over her large

39

eyes, pale blue like a Siamese cat's, her whole face freed from suffering and joy—released from life. . . . Even if he were victorious, he knew that upon his release he would go out into a world forever mutilated; he would bear this solitary death like a scar. And this alone showed him the power of that night which had him in its grasp and the power of the enemy which was able to eject him from the world of men as though he were insane or dead.

The guard's footsteps grew fainter, dully reverberating in the corridor, monotonous like all mortuary sounds.

"If I go round the cell ten times before the second guard comes (they always followed each other at short intervals) she is still alive."

He began to circle the cell. Two. Three. He bumped into the wall, miscalculating the distance. Four. "I must not go so fast. I must keep the same pace." He knew that in spite of his limp he was running. Six. The guard's step. Seven. Eight. Now he was running in the smallest possible circles, turning almost on the same spot. The guard passed.

Nine.

He lay down on the floor. Lying down was forbidden.

"If I can count to a hundred before they return, it means that she is alive."

One, two, three. . . . Silence. He closed his eyes, and the numbers followed one another as before an execution. Sixty, eighty, ninety-eight, one hundred: "Alive."

He saw Anna's eyes open, and opened his: while he was counting he had unwittingly drawn his feet together, crossed his hands on his chest, like a corpse.

"I'm already going mad," he thought.

The steps of the guards; but he decided not to get up: he wanted to see a man. His courage, like all courage, was much better able to cope with danger than with terror. He had known this since a certain night he had spent in Siberia, in a village which the Whites were hourly expected to surround; terror had come over him, but when he had had the idea of opening the doors and windows of his hut, he had gone to sleep.

The guards passed without opening the peephole. "It's difficult to kill oneself beforehand, here. . . . I simply must think of some way. If I'm tortured, I may be lucky enough to have the strength to keep my mouth shut, but if I go mad . . . To have saved the list, only to reveal things that are ten times more important! And perhaps one doesn't notice it. . . ." Perhaps one went mad by imperceptible degrees. And was he lucid at this very moment, seeking his wife's fate in numbers, as he lay stretched out in the posture of the dead?

A guard came back into the corridor, humming. Music!

There was nothing around him, nothing but a geometric hollow in the enormous rock, and in this hole a bit of flesh awaiting torture; but in this hole there would be Russian songs, and Bach and Beethoven. His memory was full of them. Slowly, compellingly, music was banishing insanity from his breast, his arms, his fingers, and from the cell. Gently it brushed over all his muscles, except those of his throat which, like his open lower lip, was unusually sensitive—although he did not sing, merely remembered. Subdued at first, gradually released, and at last soaring free, the imaginary sounds recaptured the emotions of love and childhood, the emotions which seem to concentrate man's whole being in his throat; cries, sobs, and outbursts of panic. In the silence which surrounded Kassner like the lull before a storm, over his imprisonment and his madness, over his dead wife, his dead child, his dead friends, over all the people possessed by terror, man's joy and grief rose in a mute paean.

He closed his eyes. Uneasy waves, torpid like his wounds, began to stir in the depth of his consciousness, and little by little the solemnity of the deep began to settle over them—then, as if the whole vast forest of sound had bowed at the mere motion of a

hand, the chant fell and suddenly rose again, straining at all his wounds, lifting him like a ship to the
very crest of suffering: this is the burst of music
which is always the call of love. And beneath the
pain madness lay waiting, ambushed in his members like the pain itself since he had stopped moving. He had been obsessed by the nightmare of a
vulture shut up with him in a cage, which with relentless blows of its pick-shaped beak was tearing
off pieces of his flesh, all the while staring greedily
at his eyes. The vulture was coming, long swollen
with the black blood of darkness. But music was
the stronger. It possessed Kassner completely, he
no longer possessed it: snow in Gelsenkirchen, with
a dog barking at a flock of wild ducks, whose cries
were almost inaudible in the muffling whiteness;
strike-calls shouted through megaphones at the
siren-blasts from the mines; sunflowers mowed
down in the guerrilla fighting, their yellow petals
spattered with blood; winter over Mongolia

44

blanched by a three-day storm, rose-petals shriveled like dead butterflies in the yellow wind; frogs croaking in the rainy dawn, a village with drenched palm trees, the distant horns of motor trucks still enveloped in darkness; Chinese merchants fleeing with their rattles before the Red Lancers and vanishing under the glow-worms down an avenue of palms; the limitless expanse of the Yang-Tze flood in the wan moonlight, with piles of corpses caught in the crooked tree-branches; and all those heads pressed against the cold earth teeming with insects listening for the rumble of the White army on the horizon of the steppes or the Mongolian plains—and his youth, his suffering, his very will, all was vanishing, revolving in the motionless cadence of a constellation. The vulture and the prison-cell were being submerged beneath a flooding death chant that enveloped all in a lasting communion, in which music perpetuated the whole past by liberating it from time,

45

mingling all its manifestations even as life and death merge in the immobility of the starry sky; fragments of war scenes, voices of women, shadows in flight, all memory was dissolving in an endless rain which fell over things as though it were sweeping them into the remotest reaches of the past. Perhaps death resembled this music; even here, or in the guard room, or in the dungeon at the moment when he was to be killed, perhaps his life would stretch out before him thus—without violence, without hatred, wholly submerged in solemnity as his body was now enveloped by the darkness, as these shreds of memories were flooded by these sacred harmonies. Beyond the cell, beyond time, there was a world which triumphed even over suffering, a twilight world, swept clear of primitive emotions, in which all that had made up his life glided with the invincible movement of a cosmos in eternity. With the sensation he had had in dreams of soaring on outspread wings, he now felt his lean body mingling, little by little, with the

46

boundless fatality of the stars, his whole being held spellbound by the army of the night careening towards eternity through the silence. He had a vision of the black sky of Mongolia spreading its canopy over the Tartar camel-drivers prostrate in the dust of the Gobi desert amid the fragrance of dried jasmine, the drone of their wailing chants punctuated by the nocturnal refrain . . . *and if this night should be a night of destiny—May it be blessed until the coming of dawn.* . . .

He struggled to his feet. While he remained motionless his limbs and his flesh seemed to dissolve in the darkness; the aching parts, with their denser masses, like knots in wood, only became localized when he moved. At the first step he again became excruciatingly conscious of the structure of his body, of his bones and their throbbing joints, of his head, which was larger in the darkness than it had seemed in the light; yet there was something more in music than the fatality of endless disintegration produced by sounds, causing man to sink, from

serenity to serenity, to the abject domain of con-
solations; the music now issued forth a call that was
echoed and reëchoed to infinity. In this insurgent
valley of the Last Judgment, it seemed to bind in a
common bond all the voices of that subterranean
region in which music takes man's head between its
hands and slowly lifts it towards human fellowship.

It was the call of those who, at this very hour,
were painting the red emblem and the call to vengeance on the houses of their murdered comrades,
of those who were replacing the names on street
signs with names of their tortured fellow-workers,
of those in Essen who had been beaten down with
bludgeons, and who, as they lay there, limp like
strangled men, their faces gory with the blood
which streamed from their mouths and noses, because the SA-men wanted them to sing the *Inter-
nationale*, had shouted the song with such fierce
hope ringing in their voices that the non-commis-

48

sioned officer had drawn his revolver and fired. Kassner, shaken by the song, felt himself reeling like a broken skeleton. These voices called forth relentlessly the memory of revolutionary songs rising from a hundred thousand throats (and no music is more exalting than a refrain pealed forth by a multitude), their tunes scattered and then picked up again by the crowds like the rippling gusts of wind over fields of wheat stretched out to the far horizon. But already the imperious gravity of a new song seemed once more to absorb everything into an immense slumber; and in this calm, the music at last rose above its own heroic call as it rises above everything with its intertwined flames that soothe as they consume; night fell on the universe, night in which men feel their kinship on the march or in the vast silence, the drifting night, full of stars and friendship. . . . Like his exhausted heart, it throbbed anxiously over his whole youth, over the mines on strike, over the fields of sleeping cattle

49

slowly awakened by dog barks reëchoing from farm to farm. . . . And, as the song completely subsided, the fervor of life and death just now united in the musical harmony was swallowed up in the world's limitless servitude: the stars would always follow the same course in that sky spangled with fatality, and those captive planets would forever turn in their captive immensity, like the prisoners in this court, like himself in his cell. Then, upon three repeated notes like peals of church bells, the first note bearing down upon all his wounds at once, the last shreds of the firmament receded to the depths of the world of anguish and little by little assumed the form of a vulture.

With his eyelids tightly shut, a slight fever in his hands that were now clutching his chest, he waited. There was nothing—nothing but the enormous rock on every side and that other night, the dead night. He was pressed against the wall. "Like a centipede," he reflected, listening to all this music born of his mind which now gradually was withdrawing, ebb-ing away with the very sound of human happiness, leaving him stranded on the shore.

Only a sly submissive kind of sub-human creature grown utterly indifferent to time could adapt itself to the stone. Time, that black spider, swung back and forth in the cells of all the prisoners as horrible and fascinating for them as it was for their comrades who were sentenced to die. For Kassner suffered less in the present than in an obsessing future, in a perpetual "forever" which his absolute dependency and the closed door made more penetrating than the cold, the darkness and the oppression of the stone. Something within him attempted to adapt itself, but the only adaptation possible was a state of stupor; a stupor broken by long musical phrases that lingered in the cell like stragglers. They were phrases of orthodox plain-chants, their notes so prolonged that they seemed almost stationary; with all the obsessing force of the moment when he had decided to face arrest, they insistently called up the scene in the antiquarian's shop with its Russian bric-a-brac—the ikons, stoles, chasubles, dalmatics and crosses—and finally dissolved into nothingness. This struggle against stupor and the slow hours went on relentlessly, at a tempo which was gradually decreasing, and Kassner would live through it here to infinity, with those orthodox ornaments in the depth of his obsession as if in the hold of a sunken galley, to a slower and slower rhythm, more and more drawn out, like circles in the water, until all was nullified in the silence of complete mindlessness.

Someone knocked. Was it at the cell-door?

He had been waiting for those knocks.

Another knock.

"Who is it?" he asked.

Low voices beyond the door, matter-of-fact voices, answered: "It is we." They had not come this time with arms outstretched, but as an impassive delegation sent by torture itself, its voice heavy

with death. But the tapping continued: five knocks
—two more; and each knock brought Kassner back
towards what was left of consciousness in the darkness of his cell; it was a prisoner who was tapping.

Two taps, a pause, and then six more; then a
longer pause.

No one had answered when he had knocked.
Everything that resembled hope resembled madness.

Was it not also madness to run away from all
hope?

Five taps; two; two; six; nine; ten; one, four;
one, four; two, six; nine.

But it was already a hopeless jumble. And the
intoning of those orthodox psalms persisted, a tomb-
chant over the treasure of a despoiled cathedral,
confusing all the numbers! First of all, first of all,
he must show that he was listening! He tapped.
The other would answer, and no doubt repeat his
message.

How could he write, here in the cell?

53

The other prisoner began again, more slowly this time.

Oh, to be able to write—to write! Kassner felt like stamping with his foot, like a horse, when he heard the taps again; he wanted to accompany them with his whole body. But he would forget them none the less. "I must think." But how could he think when he was permeated to the marrow by that intangible presence, by the menace of blows, by the frantic despair betrayed by the faint sound of his chattering teeth?

The other prisoner resumed his tapping:

5; 2; 2, 6; 9; 10; 1, 4; 1, 4; 2, 6; 9.

And still the interminable chant.

"I wonder what it was that they used to call torture by hope? . . ." If Kassner were in turn to tap out a message, perhaps the other could make out what he said. But how would he prepare an alphabet? The taps were about to begin again. . . .

He made one of the greatest efforts of his life to

think. He could not drive from his mind the image of a hand vainly trying to catch a fly on the wing. He managed, however, to note that the other struck thirteen figures. "If I added them up to a single number I might perhaps remember it. No. Too long. If I cut it in two? Perhaps . . ."

Silence.

He was waiting, hardly able to breathe, his whole body taut with agonizing suspense. He knocked at the wall again and again, at sheer random now. Nothing. He had not grown deaf: he heard his own knocks, his steps, the whole muttering jumble of the prison-sounds above the stubborn intoning. The guards had opened a near-by door. Had the one who was tapping just been caught or by chance simply taken from his cell? Like the music just now, hope was deserting him, was leaving him to the mercy of an annihilating stupor. Yet he continued to listen for the knock that would come; in vain; and once more hope ebbed, an illusory last time, like the illusory last spurt of blood expelled from a wound by the heart's irrepressible pulsation.

He shut his eyes, and the dimly glowing world of half-sleep settled upon him. A jumble of images through which first appeared an iridescence like that of oily water; pink finally predominated, slashed by a criss-cross of diagonal black streaks. Was it that river ford where the fish, asphyxiated by the shells of the Whites, had streamed down upon the starving insurgents with their guns slung across their shoulders, the piles of pink-bellied fish catching the cold dawn's salmon-colored light? . . . As if the sun had suddenly risen, this light turned golden and blended into the shapes of a profusion of sacerdotal jewelry like the antiquarian's. Their jagged surfaces flickered to the strains of the ghostly chant like the tiny flames of ikon lamps, and at the same time they were the night-lights of the Trans-Siberian grounded like an ocean liner in the forest under the telegraph insulators. . . .

56

Civil war.

His mind was hurtling in a dizzy race in pursuit of the images that sustained his life. He must try to organize this race, to bring it under the control of his will. When Bakunin was in prison he would edit an entire imaginary newspaper every day: the editorial, news, fiction, literary articles, society gossip. . . . The fleeting images evoked by the music had been merely spectacles; he must bring them into the realm of time. The whole problem of captivity was to cease to be passive. Perhaps Kassner would be able to overcome the stupor, the madness, and the obsession of escape that composed his subterranean life, as the hope of heaven sustains the Christian through a life of sin. There was still as much strength within him as there was menace around him.

Chapter Three

THE variegated chandler's shop-front which he saw after his arrest becomes Saint Basil's church with its many-colored onion-shaped domes at one end of Red Square; and, as if the antiquarian's crosses and censers, his whole display of stoles and dalmatics, were rising from the earth, the cupolas of a convent fortress glittering with copper stars rise in the night, with their double crosses and their rigging of golden chains covered with rooks and pigeons; below, a counter-revolutionary city cluttered with votive offerings, toys and sanctuaries, Old Russia whose blood-stained mysticism fails to conceal the corpses of the revolutionaries. The foreign battalion, sent to reinforce the troops that had been beaten back, takes cover in a wood, with a machine-gun. In the fortress there are cells. In

61

one of the cells, a prisoner. He will make his escape.
He is in a corridor; behind a grimy window, a
flower is barely visible, two spots, one red, one
green, in color, in color! He is running towards an
airplane. His wife is in Prague.

Kassner's mind was turning round and round in
the obsession of escape, like his body in the cell.
He must remember minutely, doggedly reconstruct
—not be carried away: recreate. He demanded too
much of fate to love his past, but his disintegrated
memory had recovered its strength by finding an
objective. Patiently, stubbornly, he worked back
to that wood full of anxious suspense before the
town huddled in the rift of fog.

The night presses against the wintry earth,
weighed down by a presence that slowly takes pos-
session of the entire nocturnal landscape: orthodox
crosses brandished like cudgels, Russian proces-
sional banners with their paste pearls catching reflections of moonlight, gradually loom up over
a knoll. A boar scurrying through the foliage: it is

an insurgent on the run, his mouth wide open, a blue fleck of moonlight on his eyes. A pope [1] in high ceremonial vestment appears on the hummock, clinging with all his weight to the banner pole which he has used to hoist himself; the material flutters and ripples in the breeze that has just risen.

Kassner listens for the accompanying sound. Nothing. Complete silence. And no rustle of leaves, none of the earth's nocturnal whispers. No sound accompanied the boar-like flight of the man beside him a moment ago, and that open mouth is shouting—and he does not hear it.

Deaf! He heard his own scream ringing through his brain: and the sound of the wicket which the guard had just opened. The latter looked at the prisoner, who was stunned by the light, panting in his anguish as though he were choking, shrugged his shoulders, and the deafening clatter of the

[1] A parish priest of the Greek Catholic Church.

wicket buried Kassner once more in his controlled madness.

The popes who have come up over the knoll begin to advance, with their dalmatics and tiaras under the crosses and banners, and a boundless unreality animates this marching Treasure, this goldsmith's folly let loose over the muddy fields, with all those white beards, and those trembling gleams of pearls and silver in the moonlight. They approach and in voices of whipped-up hatred they chant the psalm which has been lurking for hours in the cell, and which passes into the rustling leaves like an escaping animal and mingles with the remote tinkle of their silver trappings. The distant howling of a dog, close as the shadow of a bird gliding with outspread wings.

No: it is a prisoner howling in a neighboring cell.

Mustering all his strength Kassner fixes his eyes on a small creature, a rat or a ferret, that scurries off, heading towards the popes. They are now motionless, dwarfed by the vast lunar landscape; although their crosses look like bludgeons, they are unarmed, and it is difficult to fire on an unarmed man unless he is hiding; they are handling some small objects from which rises smoke that soon turns to dust, seeming to solidify in the wind under the moon: censers.

How long is it since Kassner has smoked? . . . The night wafts towards him an odor of churches, incongruous in this outspread landscape glazed by cold and hatred under the radiance of the great starry sky; while this dank smell settles little by little over the pungent boxwood leaves, more figures appear over the knoll, row upon row, bristling with menacing crosses. Behind them the Whites who yesterday, thanks to them, recaptured the village. The screams of a Red peasant undergoing

65

torture, in the bleak sunshine of a wintry afternoon, have lasted more than an hour. . . .

It is the prisoner in the neighboring cell who is screaming again. There are many forms of torture in the imagination of men. Kassner clamps his hands over his ears.

There is a shot from behind the crosses: one of the Whites fires; almost immediately another shot, fired by one of the popes (a revolver?); a third one gives off the same red light as the censers. And the machine-gun of the foreign battalion begins to fire. It is a little behind Kassner; he prudently draws back. It is tapping small, even blows, like a key on the bars of a cell-grill; the end of a branch shot off by a bullet falls, swept sideways by the wind. Kassner has fed this very same machine-gun in the Caucasus, he remembers the time when he had to cool it by crushing grapes over its red-hot barrel—the sizzling sound of the juice as it bubbled over the steel. A pope, the third one tonight, falls clutching several times at his cross, as though he were turning round it; the others begin to run, mingling now with the White soldiers who are catching up with them. The tempo of the machine-gun fire becomes more rapid, and shots from the old guns flash on all sides through the woods: the insurgents have seen the Whites at last—and all these deaths seem a mockery in the indifference and the great silence of the stars.

"Where are you from?" the machine-gunner asks Kassner.

"Foreign communist."

Once more silence, and the wind, and the night.

"I'm from the Altai. Look at them lying there, with their silver robes and their great white beards: why are they like the snow that lingers in the mountain clefts?"

On the night-darkened earth, the fallen bodies form the design of a great white vulture with torn wings and an enormous beak.

67

A voice in the cell articulated clearly, but in a mere whisper, the solemn words: "They are dead." And, a little louder: "Anna is also dead, I tell you. . . . She is dead." Beneath Kassner's hands, still clamped to his ears, the blood was panting, summoning images as a diver clamors for air; blood, his only living companion, full of submerged bells ringing, conscious of the earth's suffering, of rhythmic gallops in the dead of night. The walls of the cell had just come closer to Kassner; no, it was the tide of anguish rising at each peal of the bells in his temples. Back to the town, back to the town!

Is it the same convent or is it not? Its bells lost in the sky, it drifts with the dreary clouds like a phantom ship, far from its dead crew stretched out in full regalia on the frozen plains. Why watch with such fascinated attention the arm of a bearded man in a brocaded doublet who tries to catch two falling snow-flakes in his glass full of vodka, at the

68

foot of the wall over whose edge the hanged insurgents are still dangling from the great black
bells covered with fluttering rooks? He is there in
the midst of the great concentrated silence, in which
hundreds of pieces of gilt furniture transform the
main street into a chaotic drawing-room made snug
by the low sky which is now turning yellow; having captured the town at daybreak, in a great whirling movement of men and frosted leaves through
the last shreds of night, the insurgents have dragged
from the rich houses all the twisted furniture, a
fantastic assortment of baroque Russian adaptations
of Louis XV and Escargot; on the largest piano,
with feet like cathedral gargoyles, there is an enormous spray of artificial white flowers. In the midst
of all this a carnival of the bearded insurgents is in
full swing: they have stripped the popes of their
chasubles, and in the intervening few hours have
tailored the brocade into Tales of Hoffmann cos-
tumes. They make their way between the gilt and
silvered armchairs and pianos in the dim light in

which snow now begins to fall, like lunatics who have suddenly taken over an Opera house. From the ground rises a distant disquieting rumble choked by the snow. . . .

Resisting the onrush of images, Kassner concentrated on the approaching sound of this muffled pounding, its hurried beat gradually slowing down to the rhythm of a steamboat engine. Abandoning their armchairs and their dreams, the insurgents scurried into the houses. . . . A few shots, and nothing more: there was no fighting. Nothing but the rhythm of blood pounding in his temples which was now shaking the bowels of the earth, all the more distinct as it was being pierced through by furious whinnyings: the cavalry!

Here they come round the corner! Harnessed, saddled, with all their semi-Asiatic trappings, thousands of riderless horses were invading the town. With the long wave-like gallop of creatures turned wild, they wheeled into the main street, carried away by their own momentum like sails before the wind, knocking over settees and armchairs in a pandemonium of hoof beats and whinnyings. They were rushing, hurtling forward with necks stretched out in front of their foam-covered backs, crowded by the street like cattle by the entrance to a corral, as if sprung fully harnessed from prehistoric migrations. The tiny figures of the last insurgents were fleeing before this convulsed fleet whose motion rose and fell; both fleet and sea filled the street from end to end, before the dull eyes of the mangy nags stamping frantically behind their wooden fences: the fleeing Cossacks had abandoned their mounts. Covetously the insurgents watched this squandered wealth which was rushing past them in an inexhaustible stream—until finally, behind the Cossack horses, the peasant horses appeared. They had torn down their fences in the stampede. After all those trappings, these saddleless horses looked naked, with an altogether human nakedness. The

71

tight clusters of sound made by their hooves in their wild flight towards the gathering dusk, opened gradually like fans towards the woods already half enveloped in darkness. In spite of the gloom and the war crouching behind the mountains, they were the very cry of the quivering earth, joyful beneath the frost. The open air! A coldness, unlike that of prison walls, reared like one of those horses—the last of which were disappearing, with heads tossed back—rearing in the icy night, hammering the naked earth with its savage hooves, the earth that was as living as the rivers and the sea!

Kassner opened his eyes.

There was nothing with a cutting edge. Neither a rope nor a handkerchief. Open his veins with his fingernails? He found that they were not yet long enough.

Was there nothing else? A friend of his had asked that one of his veins be opened after his death, to be sure that circulation had ceased. Kassner remembered the assistant's scalpel (the doctor had refused) seeking the fine white vein in flesh that no longer bled. Thus with his bloody fingertips he would seek one of his own full and throbbing veins, without seeing it.

His body which had appeared to him so vulnerable now lived with a dully invincible animation, his heart and respiration protected by its cage of bones. "Nature acts as though men were always anxious to commit suicide. . . ."

He felt a need both to die in peace and to sink his thumbs into the throat of the first guard who entered, without letting go, no matter what happened. . . . How could he make his death useful? In this hole, it was impossible to help anyone. "To have had so many opportunities to die. . . ." How badly fate chose. He would have to fall back on his fingernails.

It would not be so very simple. He went up to the streak of light that outlined the door, and was

73

able to make out his hand with its outspread fingers, its nails which felt very short. He would use the nail of his little finger like a vaccination needle. He tried to make it penetrate his flesh, at the wrist. In vain. It was too short, but also too round, too blunt: the flesh was both more elastic and harder than he thought. He would have to sharpen the nail by rubbing it against the wall. At least two more days.

He was still trying to see his fingers, whose tips barely emerged from the total darkness as though they had belonged to a strange hand. His courage had assumed the form of death. And he looked, with fascination, at that almost invisible flesh which was his and on which the nail which would enable him to kill himself was slowly to grow.

Once more he began to pace the floor. The hand which was to be his death hung beside him like a satchel. The hour that was approaching would be the same as this; the thousand smothered sounds that teem like lice beneath the silence of the prison would repeat to infinity the pattern of their crushed life; and suffering, like dust, would cover the immutable domain of nothingness.

He leaned back against the wall, and surrendered himself to stagnant hours.

Chapter Four

THE light came from a lamp at the end of the corridor. Outside it was night, no doubt.

The guard, standing with legs apart, was examining him. This fellow is looking for some fun, thought Kassner. He had heard stories of prisoners who were made to walk on all fours.

The guard took a step forward.

Kassner was certain to meet either cruelty or the will to humiliate, and yet he could barely make out anything upon the man's features but the look of a slave buyer. He drew back a step to keep his distance, throwing his body forward and raising his left heel: if he speaks, he said to himself, I won't answer, but if he tries to touch me I'll ram my head into his belly. We'll see what happens after that.

The guard made no mistake: in the recoil of

fear the torso is held back, not forward. Something fell limply.

"Work. Unravel," he said.

The door closed.

The very moment Kassner thought he was closest to suicide, reality had sufficed to give him back his strength. Before, when the SA-men had come into his cell, all fear had left him, in spite of the screams from the neighboring cells. He knew the world of insomnia, and had been haunted by sensations of distress inexhaustibly reiterated, with an insect's precision: this was the world in which he was now struggling, and he could not expect to achieve a calm obviously beyond his reach, but he could perhaps count on his head and his fists being there, ready to strike. And he had forgotten the sense of touch so completely that he would have struck as a hungry man eats.

He went over to the object that the guard had dropped, and picked it up: it was a piece of rope.

Could one not eat a rope, well broiled? A rare

slice of roast meat, beads of water forming on the decanters, anise and mint sherbets in the evening, by the trees! How many times had he been fed since he was here? Hunger subjected him to occasional sharp spasms of disgust.

"Work. . . ."

It occurred to him that unraveling the rope would wear down his fingernails, and he thought of suicide returning to search for what it had forgotten. The metallic clicks of doors slammed shut followed one another in a rising scale in the dense black silence: no doubt the guards were distributing rope. Did the suicidal urge enter with the rope into all these holes, at its appointed hour, the same for almost all, like despair and degradation, each coming at its appointed hour? Did not the waves of madness, which had left Kassner, drag his companions into their maelstrom, lower and lower, farther and farther from the men they were? Did they not grasp the rope, did they not go mad, before that Nazi rope, on finding that their

sole gesture of liberty had been foreseen, that they
were robbed of their death, as they had been robbed
of life? . . . There were those who had been
longer in the cells than he had, and the very young,
and the sick. . . . In each cell there was a rope,
and Kassner could do nothing more than strike the
wall.

Blow after blow. He hardly dared to listen. Yet
either he had lost his mind, or something was answering. From the same direction as a while ago.
While he listened with all his might, he was afraid to
hear: would not these knocks cease once more?
Once already he had thought he heard the guard's
step and he had been mistaken. Hope itself was a
form of suffering.

Full of infinite patience, the patience of a prisoner, the invisible hand began again:

Five—two—two, six—nine—ten—one, four—one,
four—two, six—nine.

Nine was separated from ten by a longer pause
than two from six.

82

While he was knocking, Kassner had not sought the alphabet. That did not greatly matter, and the essential thing was that communication should be established: he was freeing his companion, he was freeing himself, from nothingness as effectively by listening as by knocking. The groups of two figures—two-six, one-four—no doubt did not belong to a system of dividing the alphabet, since they were followed by isolated figures. They almost surely indicated numbers. 5-2-26—9-10. He had already forgotten the others.

He knocked once more.

Once more the neighbor answered.

5-2-26; 9-10; 14-14; 26-9.

Over and over again he tapped out the numbers until Kassner had repeated them.

The latter was pressing his eyelids together with all his might, till his temples ached, trying to visualize these figures in order. It was not in their names but in their signs that the key to their meaning lay. He felt like an insect squeezed in its hollow stone,

avariciously contracting its legs over its accumu-
lated wealth—just as his fingers against his chest at
this moment were contracted over those numbers,
which were tokens of friendship and which the
weakness or the over-excitement of his memory
might blot out, like an awakening. Hanging by
some imperceptible and precarious thread in back
of his eyes, they nevertheless flooded the darkness, flowed over him as though he should have
to hold on to them to save himself, and his hands
were repeatedly missing them. He tried all the
keys; a figure added to the number of letters of
the alphabet, or else subtracted; multiplication;
division of the alphabet into sections. Thinking,
searching for figures, escaping the intolerable empti-
ness was such a relief that every obstacle, by com-
parison, seemed ridiculous. The alphabet read back-
wards? . . . He discovered that he only knew the
alphabet by heart by reading it forward.

What if the man who was knocking was crazy?

He remembered a former anarchist comrade

who, while lying sick in a military hospital, had persuaded several of those in the near-by beds to become conscientious objectors. He had been found out and afterwards moved to a bed between the wall and an insane man.

And why might not one of the guards be knocking meaninglessly, on purpose, in answer to his taps?

The knocks were beginning again. This blind, stubborn patience could only be that of a prisoner; and such care, such concentration on the manner of knocking could not be those of a lunatic.

By dint of patience he would find it! If he did not confuse the figures whose meaning he was seeking, through the successive guesses—to find himself at last stripped, naked, so near to this tireless brotherhood. . . .

And meanwhile every noise in the prison was becoming like a distant knock, and the entire prison

85

like that night-meeting in Hamburg where every
man had struck a match at his request, and all had
been able to gauge the size of the crowd by the
myriad tiny flames that flickered for a moment in
the night as far as the eye could reach. . . . He remembered a street in a workers' district near Alex-
anderplatz with its closed cigar-stores in the moonlight, on a night of battle. The communists had
just left the street and the last lights were going out
as the rumble of the police trucks was approaching.
Scarcely had the latter roared past when from one
end of the street to the other the windows hurled
their rectangles of light gashed by silhouettes down
on the sidewalks. Holding back a little because of
the bullets, the street population had appeared all
at once with its tense faces and unbidden children.

Doors opened for comrades who might have hidden in recesses. And then, as suddenly as it had
appeared, this brotherly demonstration was hidden
in obscurity: a new police truck was arriving, which

86

passed at full speed between houses again enveloped in moonlit apathy.

Hours were eaten away by the ant-like numbers, and the occasional passing of the guards. And slowly, almost accidentally, as though it had taken shape within him of its own accord, the idea came to him that 5 might very well indicate, not that 1 was the fifth letter, but that it was after five letters that the alphabet began. F would then be 1; G, 2 . . . Z, 21; A, 22; B, 23 . . . E, 26. Once more the other prisoner was knocking and Kassner listened, following the knocks one by one on his fingers and spelling:

2—G; 26—E; 9—N.[1]

Joy shook him, again outstripping his mind. He held his breath to the point of suffocation and involuntarily his fingers sank into his thighs. He stag-

[1] Genosse: Comrade.

87

gered back into the darkness, for a new sound was mingling with the knocks; the guard was approaching: slowly, calmly, indifferently, perhaps saturated with that boredom which the decomposition of the imprisoned exudes through the doors—a temporary prisoner among prisoners who would be released only by madness or death.

One, two, three, four. . . .

Certainly Kassner could hear better, from the cell, than the guard from without. Five, six. . . . But the latter was approaching, and would soon hear. Seven. . . . With his steps, time was rushing like a boiling torrent towards Kassner, was tearing out the tiniest fibres of his nerves. Eight, nine. . . . If the guard were to hear, not only would the man who was knocking be beaten, or sent to the vertical coffins—the cells in which the prisoner is forced to stand upright, but also the alphabet would be discovered. And Kassner felt himself as responsible as if the patience of the man who was knocking, the assistance which he was trying tirelessly to bring

88

him, had been caught as in a trap by his ignorance, by his clumsiness. Ten. . . . He was between the blows and the step which was approaching, which would be upon him within three seconds. . . . Even if the alphabet were the one which he imagined, how would he strike *look out*, find the letters: A, C. . . ? [1] He counted on his fingers beginning with F. It was more than 20. . . .

He raised his fist, understood immediately that he would not be heard if he knocked in this manner, bent his forefinger. . . .

The other had ceased knocking.

Had he too heard the guard? Probably: like Kassner's, his sustained attention to the knocks was no doubt ready to seize every sound. Certain rounds seemed to be made with regularity. In the now limitless silence in which nevertheless the menace of a call from the other cell remained suspended, the steps approached one by one. Kassner followed them, remained on the alert, shoulders hunched, as if set

[1] Achtung.

to repel the first sign of a call, his whole being taut with the mad straining of his will-power, as though to hypnotize his unseen fellow prisoner into silence.

The steps grew fainter.

The knocks, once more.

10 = O

While the prisoner continued, Kassner joined in:

1, 4 = S; 1, 4 = S; 2, 6 . . .

In the depths of the prison shadows, they were tapping out together that word: *comrade*, certain now that they understood each other, and yet neither of them interrupted the other; they went on to the end, each hearing both his own taps and those of the other, as they might have heard the faint coupled beating of their hearts.

Kassner wanted to say nothing that was not essential, wanted to use only such words as would cling to the innermost being of a man confined within stone walls. Before all, tell him that he was not alone, protect him from the rope which he was

90

not unraveling either, since he was knocking. Kassner chose his words, counted on his fingers: he had
to speak a language which he was still spelling out;
a little while ago the other's accompaniment had
helped him. But already he heard

T A K E   C O U R A G E

The guard was passing.

The other prisoner continued (and with the first
taps of the word WHO struck by Kassner, both
seemed to interrupt each other):

O N E   C A N. . . .

A slammed door seemed to crush the sound of
the knocks. Kassner's ear-drums were alert. He was
sure now that he could tell the direction of sounds,
and the slamming of the door came from the same
source as the knocks.

The guards had either entered his comrade's cell,
or another one near enough to make him stop
knocking. But something confused and distant, like
sounds under water, was taking place in there, was

making him tremble in the night. Another knock! No: a thud. Followed by another, more muffled. Still others, hard and full now: it was no longer the finger, it was the whole body of his comrade, assaulted in his cell, striking against that wall with the soft sound of flesh or the sharp sound of a skull, and reverberating in the shadows surrounding Kassner, who stood open-mouthed, drunk with helplessness and oppression.

He was waiting for them.

But perhaps they would not come. No doubt they had heard only the other prisoner's knocks (they had been more numerous than his); otherwise, they would have waited to hear who was answering, and already. . . .

But they did not come. Solitude was about to return. Deprived of brotherhood as he had been of dreams and hope, Kassner waited in the silence which hung over the desires of hundreds of men in that black termite's nest. He must speak for them, even were they never to hear him!

"Comrades in the darkness around me. . . ."

For as many hours, as many days as were needed, he would prepare what could be told to the darkness. . . .

Chapter Five

"Since then I don't know. . . . The dark hours run into one another. Anyway, a fortnight before I was arrested I was in Paris—at a meeting for the prisoners in Germany. Tens of thousands of our comrades, standing. In the main hall, in the first rows that have been reserved for them, the blind sing in dull voices, completely absorbed in the revolutionary songs which the other halls and the night fling back—sing with their terrible little blind men's gestures. For us. Because we are here.

"I saw the body of Lenin—in the old Hall of the Nobility. His head was even a little larger than usual, don't you see. And out in the night as far as the eye could reach there were people walking in the snow.

"After passing in front of the coffin—or before—we waited in a near-by house. When Lenin's widow arrived, looking for all the world like an old school-teacher, we understood that the deepest silence can become even deeper. There was the long wait. The anguish. And she felt that we were with her even in death.

"And with what little voice one can muster on such occasions, don't you see, she merely said—and none of us expected such words from that old communist—'Comrades, Vladimir Ilyitch deeply loved the people. . . .'

"You, my Chinese comrades buried alive, my Russian friends with your eyes gouged out, my German friends around me with your ropes, you in the next cell who have perhaps been beaten to death, what I call love is the thing that binds us together.

"I know how much strength it takes to do a good deed that counts. I also know that nothing will pay for what so many of us are suffering here, except victories. But at least, if we are victorious, every one of us will find his own life at last. And all those who have spurned the fellowship of men will know that they are alone; they will go home evenings to a room where they will still be alone; and they will carry with them the contempt and indifference of all, and the uselessness of their lives, trailing them always like a dog. And then they will go and find a woman to live with because one must live with someone; and they will go to bed together and produce children, who will also be unwanted; and at last they will go and rot with the myriad seeds that have fallen barren by the wayside. At this hour, if it is dark outside as it is here, in houses everywhere a hunted crowd is sitting or lying down in silence. For love is choice, and one has nothing to choose when one has nothing to give.

"But from those blind men in Paris to the Chinese Soviets, in every country in the world at this moment there are a few men who are thinking of us as though we were their dead children.

"I have seen. . . .

"I must go back. . . . It is difficult to speak in complete darkness.

"For twenty years my father was one of the most militant workers in Gelsenkirchen. Then my mother died. He took to drink. In the evenings he would go to meetings dead drunk, as people who have nearly starved to death have been known to get up at night to go and fetch some bread and hide it under their pillows. He would interrupt the speakers, act like a fool. . . . And then again there were times when he just sat quietly in the back of the meeting-halls. The others knew him, and when he came in they would look at him with sadness or exasperation, but they did not put him out. 'It's a distraction,' said a comrade ironically one day, not noticing that I was right behind him. . . . It was my father who gave me my political background—before all this, of course. . . . When I first began to make speeches he tried to give up alcohol, but he soon went back to it. His interruptions were like punches below the belt, and I had to put up with them through whole speeches. And it was then that I understood how closely I was linked to the revolution.

"He was working in the mine. One day when he was down there with two hundred fellow-miners, there was an explosion. The comrades on the rescue crews went below to the peals of an intolerable funeral bell. They were surrounded by flames, and in spite of their masks were unable to save even all their own men: two killed and one missing. We all volunteered for the rescue work, naturally, and before the pits we passed the extinguishers and the sand-bags to each other, to the sole accompaniment of the ambulance motor which stood ready and which waited in vain. The fire kept gradually advancing. A third rescuer was killed. This went on for forty hours. Then the inspectors and our delegates declared that carbon monoxide had completely filled the shafts, and they walled up the mine right in front of us, patiently. . . .

"I saw a play which was almost exactly like that, in Moscow, on the day of the youth celebration. Three hundred thousand marched past us. We had to cut through their ranks to get in; the show began at nine and the procession had begun at five. Between the acts we went out to smoke, and the inexhaustible stream of adolescents was still passing, waving red flags that formed a bristling sea at the level of the windows. Then we went back to the play—which was just make-believe for the others. But for me it was like going back to my youth. And between each act we went down again, and the youths were still marching past, and once more we went back to the play, which had been acclaimed far and wide, to the Caspian, and all the way to the Pacific, because it gave to work its meaning and its dignity. I remembered the bell, and the miners pressed round, alone in the indifference that reached to the very heart of the German night. . . . And when it was all over, as I watched the throng that still prevented us from getting out, it occurred to me that all these youths were less than twenty years old. And that therefore there was not a single man, don't you see, among all those who for hours and hours had been converging towards Red Square, not a single one of those men who had lived through the days of wrath. . . .

"We . . ."

Two steps in the corridor.

Without knowing why, Kassner stepped close to the door.

"We are together in the sealed mine. And our newspapers, which had no factory correspondents before, have all they want now that those who write to us run the risk of being thrown into these cells. And in spite of these dens of madness, there were five million 'No's' in the plebiscite.

"Don't you see . . ."

The door opened and the full light of the corridor burned right through to his brain. It streamed over his whole body, washed away the darkness which glued his eyelids.

"Well, are you going to make up your mind?"

He finally managed to open his eyes. Two red and green men, with yellow spots which dazzled him . . . They became khaki: the SA uniforms, with their black swastikas on the white armbands; white—an overwhelming color. . . . Kassner felt that he was being pushed outside.

They were leading him through great yellow waves of light. They knew now that he was Kassner. Should he try escape? He could barely control his movements any longer; he would neither be able to run nor to fight. And he could scarcely see clearly. "I shall become a man again just at the moment when I'm being tortured." With his speech still beating within him like fettered wings, he felt himself moving forward like a balloon, swept upward by the pungent air that filled his lungs, by the full, free steps he was taking, by the light which had turned blue, as when one removes dark glasses: the ground floor, daylight. "In an hour, perhaps, if

I have a chance, I may be able to kill one of them after all."

It was only when he found himself before a Nazi official, in the room where he had been examined on his arrival at the camp, that he understood they were not taking him to the guard-room or to the vaults. Not yet at least. Was he about to be transferred? Aside from the dark cells there were only the vertical coffins. The daylight shimmered over a face of which Kassner noted only the short bristling moustache and the thick eyebrows, and over two dark-colored individuals in civilian clothes, who looked like overcoats hanging from the wall against which they were leaning. Before them a ray of sunlight full of motes glittered like a canal in the wind. Kassner signed a register, the Nazi handed to one of the overcoats an envelope and a package with the paper torn, in which the prisoner thought he recognized his suspenders. One of the overcoats opened it.

"A cigarette lighter and a box of licorice are missing."

"They're wrapped in the handkerchief," said the Nazi.

The two men led the stumbling prisoner to a car. He could not keep from looking at the sky; his feet caught in every obstacle, and missed the sidewalk. They sat down on either side of him; the car immediately started off.

"At last!" said the first overcoat.

Kassner had a purely animal impulse to answer, although his companions obviously belonged to the Gestapo. In the clear air washed by great blue streams, there was something more than a little unreal about the thick-set man who had just spoken, with his thin moustache drooping over his prominent canines; as Kassner looked at him, his heavy features all seemed to become distorted, to turn into caricature. He resembled both a walrus Kassner had seen in Shanghai and the fat Chinese who was displaying him. Kassner knew his own mania for finding a resemblance to an animal in every face, but this face was extraordinary. The light raining down at a slant from both sides of the car continued to animate it as it trembled over fingers with convex, oddly curved nails. Blurred by the still shimmering daylight it seemed about to evaporate: the car was flinging everything behind and the other faces, too, were transformed into mobile, vulnerable, unstable images, ready to dissolve in the multicolored air. This was no dream; objects existed in all their dimensions, had their own weight; but they were not real. It was the other planet, the unknown world, the descent into the shadows.

"Well," said the walrus, "so we're going back to see the little mother?"

What "little mother," Kassner wondered. He had the strength, however, not to ask where he was being taken.

The walrus smiled, silently or ironically, his canines sharply defined now, against a blurred background of fields and autumnal trees. It seemed to

Kassner that it was these canines that spoke, and
not the mouth.

"Beginning to feel better, aren't you?" said the
walrus.

Kassner was humming—the chant of the popes—
at a joyous tempo, and finally became conscious of
it. His mind alone felt menaced: his body was free.
Perhaps the walrus would presently dissolve, the
auto disappear, and he would find himself back in
his cell. Perhaps what he was hearing had no rela-
tion to anyone or anything, and the ideas and words
were about to blend in nothingness with the flight
of trees and violet asters along the road's edge. One
part of himself, however, remained lucid and alert;
but around him, whether it was reality or dream or
death, a vast fiction called the earth was rushing
and whirling.

"At any rate," the walrus went on, "you're
lucky that he decided to give himself up."

"Who?"

"Kassner."

As an image seen through binoculars gradually brought into focus becomes increasingly clear, the officer's face detached itself from the light. Kassner suddenly recalled the scene of two Red guards sprawling on the ground at the entrance to a village—their sexual organs had been crushed between two bricks, and they lay dead in the Siberian dawn full of busy insects.

"Has his identity been established?"

"He confessed."

Silence.

"They confess a lot of things, here," said Kassner.

"You haven't suffered any ill-treatment. And that pig's head hadn't even been beaten. Up to that time, of course. In other words, he confessed freely."

The officer knit his thin eyebrows.

"They all knew we were looking for him. And

109

they knew we would do what was necessary to find him. Yes—whatever was necessary. We had begun. But he gave himself up."

"Whatever was necessary. . . . And what if he's a fellow who wanted the others to be spared?"

"Really? A communist! I don't think he knew about the others being punished. It was when he found out they were looking for him that he gave himself up. In other words, you're in such a stew about getting out that it makes you batty. . . ."

Had he succumbed to madness at last? This low gray dream-sky, this walrus-faced man, this trembling universe continually on the point of dissolving; and this wind-shield which reflected a hairy face which he did not recognize as his own, at the very moment when he was obliged to speak of himself as someone else. . . .

"There are the photos, I believe. And he knew what he was risking," the walrus went on.

"Where is he?"

The officer shrugged his shoulders.

"Dead?"

"I'd be surprised if he was altogether alive. . . . From the way you ask questions, I wonder how the hell they got the idea you might be an important communist. In other words, he was a son of a bitch, but not a fool."

The car passed in front of a station. Some prisoners were working on the road-bed; a man and a woman were embracing beside a train which was about to leave, and almost all the prisoners were watching them.

"He wasn't a son of a bitch."

"If you had gotten it instead of him, I suppose you'd still think he was a fine fellow?"

Kassner was looking at the man and woman who were embracing.

"If I . . . Yes."

The other officer put his hand on Kassner's arm:

"Look here, if you're anxious to go back . . ."

But the walrus, with a rapid gesture, tapped his head with his finger.

That fellow either gave himself up so they would not torture the others, thought Kassner, or else because he wanted to kill himself, or in the hope of freeing a comrade whom he considered more useful than himself: me. . . . When one is mad, is one really convinced that one isn't? A man had perhaps died in his stead; he knew it, thought about it, and was not able to become fully conscious of it; suffering as great torment as if they were torturing his child to make him talk. Even while he was asking questions he was not able to arouse himself from the nightmare of the cell.

"You don't happen to have his picture?"

The officer again shrugged his shoulders and made a gesture of indifference.

What if it were not madness, but deception?

What if all this was fabricated by the walrus, to make him talk? Or for pure pleasure? Since Kassner had left the camp he had not felt himself in the realm of truth for a moment. But did he know yet what truth was?

"And if you didn't have connections with people whom a stranger has no right to meet—if he has any respect for hospitality," said the other officer, "nothing would have happened to you. It was lucky for you that your legation looked into your case. They made a big mistake, though!"

Yes, the anti-Nazis were not without friends in the Czecho-Slovak legation.

Kassner looked at the man who had just spoken: his eyes had at last become accustomed to the light. A perfect policeman's mug, oddly combined with the correct appearance of a petty-bourgeois. But if Kassner's eye-sight had become almost normal again, his mind remained attached to the cell by a thousand delicate spider-webs. Did the walrus feel he had said too much? He had turned his head away and was looking at the fields swept by the whirl of leaves.

. . . The Polizei-Presidium at last, where after

113

various small speeches and formalities, a clerk with a bad cold handed Kassner his package (suspenders, shoe laces, etc.) and the marks that had been taken from him:

"I am keeping eleven marks seventy."

"For the stamps?"

"No: for the camp. One mark thirty per day."

"That's dirt cheap! Was I there only nine days?"

Kassner was getting back to earth; but the idea that he had been in the cell only nine days separated him once more from the world; reality was like some language he had known and forgotten by turns. And it came to him violently that his wife had just had an extraordinary stroke of luck, as though it were she who had been freed, and not he.

"That leaves you two days to get out of Germany. Unless between now and then . . ."

"Between now and then, what?"

The sniffling clerk answered nothing. Not that it mattered much. Kassner knew perfectly well that until he crossed the frontier he was not safe.

How was it that the Nazis had accepted the identity of the one who had given himself up? They had the guarantee of death, and perhaps strong and unusual reasons that he would never know. Whoever the man was, had he been killed before the documents reached the camp where Kassner was held? If it was Wolf, he would have had no trouble obtaining papers in Kassner's name; but he did not resemble Kassner. . . .

Kassner looked up, above the roofs, to the low, heavy sky: the airliners probably had not left the airdrome. He must take advantage of the expulsion, leave Germany as soon as possible to change his identity. He and the Gestapo would meet again —later. His glance dropped again, gradually, to the ground. A man had perhaps died in his stead. In the street, the life of every day continued.

Would the factory plane be able to leave?

Chapter Six

THE pilot had thought he recognized Kassner in the anonymous person he was to transport, but he had asked him no questions. The small propeller factory owned by the party's clandestine organization allowed him to make several trial flights every week and to have two planes at his disposal. This one would return in a month with a different number, flown by a different pilot. Kassner withdrew his gaze from the marvelously rose-colored ham in the sandwich he was holding, and picked up the meteorological bulletin: poor visibility 10 kilometers from the field; hail-storm over the Bohemian mountain-range, a very low ceiling; a ground-fog in many localities.

"Do you get it?" asked the pilot.

Kassner was quite aware of the comradeship implied in the smile which animated his restless sparrow face at the prospect of such a journey. (Is it true, he wondered, that pilots always resemble some bird?):

"I was an observer during the war, don't you see," he said. "Have the airliners left?"

"No. The south-bound planes have orders not to leave the airdromes."

"That's the German planes. What about the Czech?"

"They haven't gone out either. Only one chance out of three of getting through."

Again Kassner gazed at this man, of whom he knew nothing except his devotion to the revolution, and with whom he was going to risk his life. He had a great capacity for friendship; and yet it stirred him even more deeply to feel that they were united not in their persons but in their common devotion, as if each step towards the machine were bringing him nearer to an austere and powerful friendship of a sort rare on this earth.

"If worst comes to worst," said Kassner, "I'd rather crash over the frontier."

"Right!"

They continued to walk towards the plane, squatting on the landing field. How small and flimsy it looked. . . .

"We start northward," said the pilot; "in weather like this we'll be out of sight in ten minutes."

They had reached the machine: a single motor, the gasoline tank very low. A week-end plane.

"Have you got a wireless?" asked Kassner.

"No."

For that matter he hardly cared.

The last stamps on the passports and documents, the parachutes attached.

"All set?"

"All set."

He turned on the ignition.

The throttle.

The plane took on altitude. Kassner could not even see the trees move, while the plane rose and fell in the head wind, with the prolonged pitching of a battleship. Far down, below some scattered clouds and birds in flight (the latter close to the earth, almost pinned to it like the human figures), the smoke of a train, lost to sight in the spacious autumn beneath the vast calm of the afternoon, spread itself over somnolent villages and blended in the distance with the dust-haze of the city. Soon there was nothing under the heavy blanket of the sky but scattered flocks of birds poised in almost submarine repose close to the earth; tree-shaded hamlets suggested a peace far removed from prisons. And yet, within this very horizon there was no doubt a concentration camp; with the relentless cruelty of children, men were torturing other men to the last extremity of suffering. Only the memory of the prison darkness enabled Kassner to realize the surrounding immensity, and the portentous land-scape banished every image except those of suffering and cruelty, as if they alone in man were as old as the woods and the plains. But above the plains and the clouds there was the alert face of the pilot. Common experience joined the two men like an old and tested friendship; the pilot was there, sharply etched on the increasingly blank background—like the answer of those whom Kassner had saved by destroying their names, like the answer of the shadows to whom he had addressed his speech; and the silent throngs of his comrades who had filled the darkness of the prison seemed to people this region of fog, the immense gray universe inhabited by the obstinate motor, more responsive than a living creature.

The plane had risen from one thousand to two thousand meters; it was now entering a bank of fog. Beneath Kassner's distraction an inner vigilance kept listening to the motor, watching for the first rift in the fog through which the earth would again spring forth. He had found only a small-scale map in the fuselage, and the thickness of the clouds made observation impossible. In the midst of the fog, which was now constant, time was disappearing in the strange sleep-like struggle. When they emerged would he find Germany, or Czecho-Slovakia, or one of those Asiatic landscapes over which he had flown so often, with their scattered imperial ruins abandoned to the wasps, and donkeys' ears quivering in the wind from the poppy fields. . . . The compass does not indicate the drift of a plane caught in a head wind. After a long stretch of solid fog, where the map barely indicated a group of hills, some vertical snow-covered crests suddenly loomed, under a sky which was turning blacker and blacker.

The plane, which had reached the altitude of the peaks, had been carried at least one hundred kilometers out of its course.

Before the immense black cloud, no longer calm and motionless in the distance, but crouching right before them, alive and murderous, Kassner became once more acutely conscious of his infinite smallness. Its edges were advancing towards the plane as if to encircle it, and the immensity, the slowness of the movement made it seem as if what was about to happen was some astronomical fatality rather than a struggle of earthly creatures. The wings nevertheless plunged into the cloud at full speed, and its yellowish and gray periphery of frayed edges, like headlands jutting into a mist-covered sea, was blotted out in a limitless gray universe, unbounded because it was separate from the earth. The dark wadding of the cloud had slipped under them, and tossed them into the domain of the sky, which was closed, banked by the same leaden mass. It suddenly seemed to Kassner that they had been released from gravitation, that they were suspended with their comradeship somewhere among the worlds, caught in the clouds in primitive combat, while the earth and its prison cells, which they would never meet again, continued their course beneath them. The frantic clinging of the tiny mechanical contrivance to the unbridled clouds, in the darkness surrounding the fuselage on all sides, was growing increasingly unreal, and at the same time all sensations were being submerged beneath the primitive voices of the hurricane.

The plane was being lifted by the wind-blasts and dropped as on a hard floor, but Kassner would have paid attention to nothing but the dogged motor which was pulling them forward, if he had not heard a sudden sizzling sound: they were in the midst of hail.

"Czecho-Slovakia?" shouted Kassner.

Impossible to hear the answer. The metal plane resounded like a drum above the crackling of the hail-stones on the windows of the fuselage: they were beginning to sift through the cracks in the cowl into their smarting faces and their eyes. Through flickering eyelids Kassner could see them stream down along the panes, bounce against the metal grooves and disappear. If a pane were to break it would become impossible to steer. And yet it seemed as though the pilot saw nothing, as though he were steering purely by instinct in the midst of the hail. Kassner nevertheless braced the window-frame with all his might and held it steady with his right hand. The inscriptions in the cells,

126

the screams, the knocks on the wall, the craving for revenge were with them in the fuselage against the hurricane.

Their course was still due south; but the compass was beginning to point east.

"Left!" bellowed Kassner. In vain. "Left!"

He could barely hear his own voice; it was almost silenced by the flying hailstones that whipped the plane into spasmodic leaping. With his free arm he pointed to the left. He saw the pilot push the joystick as if to bank 90°. Immediately he looked at the compass: the plane was going to the right. The controls no longer responded.

Yet it still seemed as if the plane were plunging into the squall with the sureness of a drill; in the midst of the uproar, in spite of the ineffectiveness of the controls, the constancy of the motor still gave the illusion of human domination. All at once the plane shuddered from end to end and ceased to move forward. The hail and the black fog were unchanged; and the compass, which alone connected them with what had been the earth, was slowly turning towards the right; then it made a complete turn. Two. Three. In the center of the cyclone the plane was spinning on its own axis.

And still the sensation of stability was the same, the motor seemed to be making a frenzied effort to pull them out of the cyclone. This turning dial was more important than all other functions; like the eye of a paralytic who has lost control of everything but his sight, it seemed to indicate that the plane was alive. Its delicate movement transmitted to them the vast fabulous life which was shaking them as it shakes trees, and the cosmic fury was refracted with precision on its minute sensitive surface. The plane continued to spin. The pilot was clutching the joystick, his whole attention riveted to the controls. But his face was no longer the worried sparrow face of a while back; it was a new face, with smaller eyes, fuller lips; by no means distorted—quite as natural, in fact, as the other. Not a deformed expression, but a new one.

And yet not surprising; as if the other had implied it, Kassner finally recognized the look of childhood—and it was not the first time (although he first now became conscious of it), that he had seen resolution in a moment of danger superimpose the features of childhood upon a man's face. The pilot jerked the joystick towards him, and the bucking plane swooped vertically; the compass dial jammed into the glass. They were caught from below, turned over like a sperm-whale by a tidal wave. Still the same regular beating of the motor, but Kassner's stomach seemed to sink through the seat. Were they climbing or looping? He recovered his breath between two new whipcracks from the hail. He noticed with surprise that he was trembling; not his hands—he was still holding the pane—only his left shoulder. He had barely begun to wonder if the plane was once more horizontal when the pilot pushed the joystick forward and shut off the motor.

Kassner was familiar with the maneuvre: let the plane drop, take advantage of the weight of the fall to pierce through the storm and attempt to straighten out the plane close to the ground. The altimeter registered 1850; but he knew that altimeters cannot be altogether relied on. Already 1600; the needle was swinging wildly, as the compass-dial had done a moment ago. If the mist reached all the way down to the ground, or if the mountains were still beneath them, they would crash. It occurred to Kassner that only the proximity of death entitles one to get sufficiently close to a man to know that child-like look which he had just seen, and that this man too was about to die for him. But at least he would die with him. Since the plane had ceased to be purely passive in the combat, his shoulder had stopped trembling; all his senses were now centered, in a manner that was definitely sexual: they were plunging with their whole weight, breathlessly, puncturing the sheet-like squalls, down through the eternal doomsday fog violently alive with the ripping sound of the hailstones.

1000

950

920

900

870

850—he could feel his eyes popping from his head, frantically fearing the approach of the mountain—and yet he was at the peak of exaltation.

600

550

500

4 . . . The plain! Not horizontal and straight ahead of him as he had expected, but in the distance and sloping. He hesitated before the unreality of this horizon slanting away at a 45° angle; but almost immediately he understood that the plane was dropping diagonally, and already the pilot was attempting to bring it under control. The earth was far away, beyond that sea of dingy clouds, like wisps of dust and hair, now closing in on them, now clearing away; a hundred meters beneath the

131

plane a leaden landscape emerged from its last shreds, black streaks of hard hills around a pallid lake which branched into tentacles that reached up the valley and reflected with a strange geological calm the low, colorless sky.

"Czecho-Slovakia?" shouted Kassner once more. "Don't know. . . ."

As if half stunned, the plane seemed to be crawling beneath the storm barely fifty meters above the crests, then over the purple vineyards and the lake, less calm now than it had seemed at first. The surface of the water rippled in the scudding wind. For the second time Kassner had the impression that it was his wife who had just been saved. The plane was passing beyond the far shore of the lake, and all that was sacred in man—the conquest of the earth —suddenly rose towards Kassner from the fields and the roads, from the factories and farms flattened by the distance, from the rivers branching into veins over the recaptured plains. The stubborn world of men was alternately exposed and obliterated by the low flying clouds; the conflict against the earth forever gorged with the dead and now taking on a more and more leaden hue was calling to Kassner in the same tone of inexorable mastery as that of the cyclone which they had passed through; and the determination of his comrades yonder, beyond the Carpathians, bent upon its subjugation, rose towards the last russet gleams in the sky with the sacred voice of infinity—with the very rhythm of life and death.

He let go the pane that he had been bracing, and smiled upon seeing once more the long life-line in the palm of his hand and the line which he had made one day, ironically, with a razor; the lines which marked his destiny had been made, not with the stroke of a razor but with patient and steadfast determination; what was man's freedom but the knowledge and the manipulation of his fate? Upon this earth, where the increasingly numerous lights seemed to rise from the autumn mist that was beginning to melt into the night, upon this earth of prison-cells and sacrifices there had been heroism; there had been holiness, and there would perhaps at last be simple consciousness. The roads, rivers, and scar-like canals were barely visible now in the mist. They were like the gradually effaced network of wrinkles on an immense hand. Kassner had heard that the lines of the hand become obliterated after death. He had looked at the palm of his mother's hand, after she died, cherishing this last lingering manifestation of life: although she was scarcely more than fifty, and her face and even the back of her hands had remained young, it was almost an old woman's palm, with its fine deep lines crisscrossing with infinite intricacy like all destinies. And the image of that hand now seemed to blend with all the lines of the earth, they too becoming obliterated by the mist and the night and assuming the features of fatality. Serenity rose up from the still leaden earth towards the exhausted plane pursued by the streaming rain as by an echo of the hail and the hurricane which it had left behind; an immense peace seemed to flood the recaptured earth, the fields and the vineyards, the houses, the trees that were perhaps full of sleeping birds.

Kassner's gaze met that of the pilot. The latter was smiling sheepishly, like a school-boy who has just escaped punishment; he had recognized one of the railroad lines and was following it through the last shifts of wind, like a great bumblebee.

On the horizon the lights of Prague were shining.

Chapter Seven

HE could hardly convince himself that he was walking on a real sidewalk, and that none of the streets of this city led to a German cell! His sharpened senses lent to the dazzling jumble of the shop-windows he was passing the fancifulness of scenes he had imagined as a child after seeing fairy-plays—great streets full of pineapples, pastry and Chinese objects in which a devil had decided to combine all the trafficking of Hell. . . . It was he who had come from Hell, and all this was simply life. . . . He got out of the car that had brought him from the airdrome.

The pilot had wanted to remain on the aviation field. He was leaving for Vienna with another comrade the next morning. Kassner and he knew all about these relationships which involve one completely and which never rise to the surface of daily life; they had shaken hands with a resigned smile.

Kassner was returning to civilian life as to a vacation in which he would be carefully sheltered from the contingencies of everyday experience; and yet he still could not recover his sense of familiarity with himself or with the world. Behind some curtains, a woman was carefully ironing clothes, was working diligently; there were shirts, and linen, and hot irons in this strange place which is called the earth. . . . And hands, too (he was passing in front of a glove shop), hands which were used for all sorts of purposes: in all that surrounded him there was nothing which had not been grasped or shaped by them. The earth was peopled with hands, and perhaps they could have lived alone, acted alone, without men. In vain he tried to recognize those objects—neckties, suitcases, candies, cooked meats, gloves, drugs—that furrier's window with a small white dog disporting himself among dead skins, sitting down, getting up again: a living creature, with long hair covering his body and with clumsy movements, that was not a man. An animal. He had forgotten about animals. The dog was moving about quite calmly in the midst of death, like all the passers-by—food for prison cells and cemeteries—walking towards the square. On large music hall bill-boards some Prussian-blue figures were prancing. The motions of the passers-by seemed to be mimicking their antics, and beneath all this, like a subdued sea, stretched the domain whose reëchoing reverberations Kassner still carried within him. His stupor was difficult to throw off. More food-shops and clothes-shops; a window full of fruit. O magnificent fruit, full of all the breath and savor of the earth! First of all he must find Anna. He entered a cigar-store nevertheless, bought some cigarettes, lit one immediately and, through the smoke, found the same unreal world: a modiste's shop, a window full of fancy leather goods, a watchmaker's (they were selling hours, too . . . the hours outside the prison cells), a café. People.

They still existed. They had continued to live, while he had gone down into the kingdom of the blind. He watched them with the mingled feelings that had seized him on one occasion during the war when he had stumbled upon a show-window full of curios at the end of a plastered hall spattered with blood. The workers' district here adjoined the poorer bourgeois quarter. . . . Was he among his own people, or among adversaries—or were these merely indifferent? There were those who were glad to be together, in half-friendship and half-warmth, and those who tried, patiently or vehemently, to extract a little more consideration from those with whom they were sitting, and all those weary feet on the floor, and under the tables hands with fingers interlaced. Life.

The tiny life of men; but there, right close to the door, three women were standing; one of them was beautiful, and her look reminded him of Anna. There were also women on the earth; but weakness had rendered him indifferent, not obsessed. Yet he felt an urge to touch them, as he had felt an urge to caress the dog: in nine days his hands had become almost dead. And behind him, somewhere, men were screaming in prison-cells, and a man had given himself up for him. Oh, how absurd to give the name of brothers to those who are merely of the same blood! He plunged into the tepid swarm of meaningless phrases, exclamations, mere respirations, as into the stupid and marvelous heat of life; he was drunk with humanity. If he had been killed that morning, perhaps his dream of eternity would have been this damp autumnal hour which little by little seemed to exude human life as beads of water form on ice-cold glasses. The theater of the earth was opening with the great festival of nightfall, the women standing round the shopwindows with their perfume of idleness. . . . O peace of evenings free from prison-cells, in which no one near by is dying! Would his ghost return here on an evening like this after he had really been killed?

Yonder in the night was the whole sleeping country-side, and the tall straight apple trees in the center of their rings of dead apples, and the mountains and the forests and the slumber of creatures over half the earth; and here, this crowd engulfing itself in life with its nocturnal smiles or plunging into death with its wreaths and its coffins; this mad, heedless crowd which did not hear its own response to the challenge of death lurking up there in its starry plains; which did not even know its own voice, its own convulsive heart submerged beneath the stir and rumble of its teeming life, to which Kassner was returning, as he was about to rejoin his wife and his child.

He had reached his house. He began to climb the stairs. Would he find himself back in his cell? He knocked at his door; no answer; knocked harder, and saw a card in the lower corner of the door: "I am at Lucerna." Anna was doing militant work among the German exiles; and Lucerna was one of the largest meeting-halls in Prague. He would have to buy the party paper. He stared stupidly at the door, forlorn and yet relieved: she had surely heard of his arrest, and he had never been able to think without anguish of the moment they would meet again. Was not the child asleep behind this confounded door? No, his knocks would have awakened it. Besides, she would not have left it alone.

When he had been set free, and later, when the plane had come out of the storm, it had seemed to him that it was she who had been saved and not he; and he felt cheated at not finding her. He went down again, bought the newspaper: Theaters. . . . Moving Pictures. . . . Lucerna: *Meeting for the imprisoned anti-Fascists*. There were meetings every week. There, too, she was with him.

The atmosphere of the meeting reminded Kassner both of a world-championship match and a village fair. At the same time it was full of menace. Fifteen to twenty thousand men were massed together, surrounded by police-forces with gleaming weapons who stood in clusters on the street corners. As the central hall was not large enough, loud-speakers had been set up all around: Kassner, who had difficulty in getting in, was surrounded by up-turned faces, absorbed in the great rasping voice of the megaphones:

". . . My son was a worker. Not even a socialist. He was sent to the Oranienburg camp and died there."

A woman's voice. When Kassner was able to reach the large hall, he made out, in the center of a row of scarlet calico strips covered with inscriptions, an aged figure awkwardly leaning over the microphone: a commonplace hat, a black coat—her Sunday clothes. A little below, a sea of heads and necks, all alike: he would never find Anna in such a crowd.

146

"Because he went to an anti-Fascist demonstration, just before the others had seized power.

"I had never taken any interest in politics. They say it's not women's concern. Their concern is dead children.

"I . . . I . . . am . . . not going to make a speech. . . ."

Kassner recognized, in her hesitancy, the distress of a person not accustomed to speaking to crowds, paralyzed after the first exhilaration has spent itself and begins to ebb, crushed by the exaltation of the crowd (besides, many of the auditors did not understand German), as though the speaker were reeling under the weight of a silent response. And yet this pause had the force of the suddenly stifled cry of slaughtered animals: the crowd, resolved not to fall back upon itself, was straining forward, panting even more than the woman; it seemed as though its own consciousness was struggling up there on the platform. Kassner thought of the street where this

147

panting was transmitted only by the loud-speakers—
and where, perhaps, Anna was listening to it. He
had come up behind the platform, was within three
yards of it, and he grew dizzy as he looked for her
among these thousands of faces, which were now
before him.

"Tell them that it's not going to happen that
way," whispered the other woman on the platform.

As at school, she was prompting. With the
crowd, her chin raised, she was waiting for the
words that seemed to stick in all their throats. The
other woman did not move, and Kassner kept his
eyes fixed on the stolid back of the speechless old
Fury whom they were prompting with words of
vengeance. By the distress registered on the faces
he guessed that she could no longer find her words.
She was bending over little by little as if she had
to wrench them from the ground.

"They killed him . . . that's what I want to tell
everybody. . . . The rest . . . the delegates, the

148

learned men who will speak . . . will explain to you. . . ."

She raised her fist to shout "Red Front" as if she had often seen this done; but, utterly abashed, she managed merely to raise a timid arm, and spoke the two words as though she were reading off a signature. They were all with her; her awkwardness had been their own, and while she was retiring to the back of the platform the helpful applause rose towards her as her grief had gone out to them. Then the excitement broke into a hum of coughs and a flourish of handkerchiefs, and while the president translated into Czech, the reaction came, the release, the anxious search for gayety. When, Kassner impatiently wondered, would the stir and confusion die down sufficiently to allow him to find Anna's eyes, which used to remind him of Siamese cats? Suddenly, some twenty meters away, he recognized her vaguely mulatto-like face, her eyes with their clear pupils entirely filling the space between the long lashes. He began to weave his way between the backs and chests; an unknown young woman was saying.

". . . forbidden him to play war, and the last time he came home with a black eye he explained: 'you see, now we are more civilized, we play revolution. . . .' " He continued to press forward step by step, fearful of projecting Anna's face on all those who remotely resembled her.

"We can surely collect funds if we get some of the fellows from the building trades on the delegation."

"Why not?"

It was very hot. His eyes were so saturated with faces that he wondered whether he would still recognize his wife. He came back towards the platform. A secretary was dictating instructions for the campaign to a comrade:

"We must keep the telephones of the ambassadors and consuls constantly ringing with demands for the release of the prisoners.—Establish headquarters.—Form investigation committees in Ger-

many.—Post-office employees, put the Thaelmann
stamp on all mail to Germany.—Sailors and long-
shoremen, continue to protest the flying of the
Hitler flag in all ports, fraternize with the German
sailors.—Railroad workers, write our slogans on the
cars bound for Germany. . . ."

Finally, the president's voice, in a conversational
tone:

"William Schradek, aged seven, has lost his father, who will find him in the office," and in a
louder voice: "We now give the floor to comrade . . ."

A name, and then a sentence which Kassner
did not understand: the commotion had suddenly died down, and around each center of noise
spread great circles of silence which little by little
drowned the applause.

"Comrades, listen to that other applause, which
rises from the depth of the night.

"Listen to its volume, how far it has travelled.

"How many of us are there in all these halls,

standing closely packed? Twenty thousand. Comrades, there are more than one hundred thousand men in the camps and prisons of Germany. . . ."

Kassner would not be able to find Anna again; and yet, in that crowd, he was with her. The little bald-headed speaker, an intellectual, judging by his vocabulary, spoke without any other gesture than that of pulling his drooping moustache. No doubt the political delegates were to speak last.

"Our enemies spend millions for their progaganda: we must do with our will what they do with their money.

"We have won Dimitrov's freedom. We shall win the freedom of our imprisoned comrades. Men rarely kill for pleasure, and these imprisonments have a meaning. They are an attempt to intimidate all the forces which oppose the Nazi government.

"But it happens that this government has to reckon with foreign public opinion. Excessive unpopularity is harmful to armament and harmful to loans.

"We must make Hitler lose by our constant, stubborn unremitting exposures more than he gains by maintaining what he calls the repression."

Kassner was thinking of his speech to the shadows.

"It is imprudent to try Dimitrov openly before the world, because it makes it necessary to show him—and to acquit him. The Cologne prosecutor has said: 'Justice has found its sword, and the executioner has seized his axe as in former days.' But he has no occasion to rejoice. Its blade makes known to all the faces of the unknown militants it reflects. With Thaelmann and Torgler, with Ludwig Renn and Ossietsky, they are advancing day after day with the sureness of all life towards death, towards what has been in all ages greatest in man. . . ."

Far beyond the spoken words, the faces seemed to express the oneness of the crowd with the men of the prison-cells. Just as Kassner had seen the pilot assume the childlike mask of a man clutched by death, he saw the faces of the crowd become transformed, and before this multitude, its elements fused into a single will, he recaptured the passions and the truths which are given only to men gathered together. It was the same exaltation as at the take-off of the war-squadrons, when the plane swept across the field between two others, pilots and observers intent upon the same combat. And this whole fellowship, at once bewildered, grave and grim, in which he was beginning to come to himself, seemed to merge with his thoughts of his invisible wife.

"German comrades, you who have brothers or sons in the concentration camps, this very night, this very minute, from this hall as far as Spain and all the way to the Pacific, crowds like ours are gathered, and our watch extends across the whole world. . . ."

These people had chosen to come here, and not seek pleasure or sleep, because they wanted to give courage to those entombed in the prisons of Germany; they had come because of what they knew

and did not know, and in their unbreakable determination, which surrounded Anna also, could be
found their reply to the challenge of that body
beaten to death against the wall of the cell and to
the unceasing voice of man's suffering that rose up
out of the earth. All were waiting for the slogans.
Kassner had wondered many times, remembering
those two Siberian corpses with their testicles
crushed and butterflies fluttering around their faces,
what value there could be in thinking. No human
speech went so deep as cruelty. But man's fellowship could cope with it, could go into the very
blood-stream, to the forbidden places of the heart
where torture and death are lurking. . . .

Chapter Eight

H<small>E</small> lit a cigarette, the twelfth since the airdrome, as if to light the stairway which was now in darkness. The door to his apartment stood ajar. He pushed it open, and went in. No one in the study, but a sound of voices in the second room, though no light filtered through under the door. The shutters had not been closed. He listened, with one finger on the switch, to the voice which seemed to be muffled by the obscurity and clarified by the reflections from the street in the dark study where a hanging made a great pale shadow:

"My little springtime . . . my lamb . . . my chick! I have given you lovely eyes—such blue eyes!—and if you're not satisfied I'll give you Sunday eyes. With them, we'll go and see the land of little animals. Where there are dogs and birds, all in plush because they're so young; and boy fish and girl fish, whose lights are like dandelions, except that they're blue. And we'll see kittens and bear-cubs. On tip toe. The two of us."

But her voice changed as if she had been struck, and sorrowfully she repeated:

"Only the two of us. . . ."

The child answered with little cries. On the other side of the door, Anna was also in darkness, and Kassner's heart was filled with love for her and the child.

"You will see the sad fish who live deep down in the sea. They have lanterns to light their way. And when they are too cold . . ."

She hesitated.

"They run away to the land of the fur-coated fish," said Kassner in a low voice as he pushed open the door.

She had clutched the back of her chair and was nervously shaking her head as if to deny both Kassner's arrival and the existence of fur-coated fish. He was smiling with a paralyzed smile which he felt drawing the skin on his face like a wound that is closing. The shadow from the window formed on Anna's bosom a great black cross that shook as she trembled; and Kassner could see that under her skirts her knees were shivering like shoulders. She got up, still clinging to the back of her chair as if she were tied to it. She finally let go of it, reached for the switch, but did not dare to touch it; he felt that she was afraid of seeing his face in the light. Words and gestures were absurd and false, above all ridiculous, more violent and less deep than their feelings—they were almost parodies. Only silence and that common immobility that was stronger than an embrace would have been appropriate; but neither of them dared, and they fell into each other's arms.

"Tell me—what was it like?" she asked when she drew away from him.

"Terrible," he said simply.

He caressed the child's head, and felt the cheek

that sought his hand. He hardly knew the features of the little face. All he remembered was its expressions, and before its first smile on the eve of his departure the child's existence had had no tangible reality for him. That life filled him with buoyant hope, but above all he treasured the absolute, animal confidence which the child had in him. One day when he had slapped his fingers for pulling the dog's coat, the child had sought refuge in *his* arms. Weighted with slumber, the soft cheek tilted into his hand; it seemed to express the completeness of the child's trust, which extended even to its dreams. For him alone Kassner was a world of joy. "Yesterday, at this hour . . ." Kassner gently withdrew his hand, passed it before his eys and made out the five fingers in the limpid darkness. Had his nails grown, he wondered? They passed into the study. She turned to him:

"Did they accept the false identity, at the . . ."

He had just turned on the light. Instinctively she had drawn her shoulders back; but no:

"I was so afraid that . . ." she said.

By the glow of the cigarette, he had seemed ema-
ciated. As a matter of fact the loss of flesh changed
his bony face very little. And she was familiar
enough with letters from wives of prisoners who
could not recognize their husbands, from those who
were told "Bring some clean linen" because the
shirt he had on was filthy with blood . . . "He
had been so frightened."

"They accepted your false identity?" she asked a
second time.

He felt that these questions were recurring in
his presence as they had recurred day after day during Anna's solitude.

"No. That is, not at the beginning. Afterward,
some other man claimed that he was Kassner."

She raised her eyes in a silence so explicit that
he was able to answer:

"No, I don't know who. . . ."

She sat down on the couch, near the window.
She was silent, and she looked at him as though a

163

part of himself had remained in death with the one who had given himself up.

"Killed?"

"I don't know. . . ."

"I have so many things to tell you," she said; "but right now I can't—not yet. I need just to talk, about anything that comes into my head . . . to get used to the idea that you are with me once more. . . ."

He knew that he should take her in his arms in silence, that only this could express what was between them and their dead comrade, but he was not in the mood for the old gestures of affection, and there are no others.

"How is he?" asked Kassner, nodding towards the room where the child had fallen asleep.

She answered with a motion of her head that expressed both melancholy and wonder; as if all the radiance she could muster would have been vain, as if the sound of her voice could not have ex-

164

pressed her love for the child without carrying with it the pain of her other love.

In the five years that they had lived together, it was the first time that Kassner had come back from such a long journey; but he knew what these returns in the shadow of a future departure were to her. This suffering which made her cling to him with eyes full of desire for congeniality, for gayety —yes, this suffering which he was causing her separated him from her atrociously. And the fact that she approved of his departure, with her mind and her heart, the fact that she was doing party work to the extent of her ability, made no difference. He sometimes wondered if in her innermost consciousness she did not reproach him for his life in which there was something that took no account of her suffering—a suffering she scarcely admitted but bore with humiliation and despair. He was not unaware of how much he himself sometimes begrudged her his own love.

"When the plane left the ground, there were whirls of leaves below us. Joy is always a little like that—whirling leaves . . . fluttering on the surface. . . ."

There was a certain cruelty in denying joy at the very moment when she wished to be the embodiment of his joy; but she had guessed the attunement to her grief which his words implied, and nothing that united them made her suffer:

"If only I could give you joy . . ." she said.

She felt his uneasiness, and shook her head with a sadness so delicately calculated in its very awkwardness that he realized once again how crude a man always is in matters of love.

"My life is what it is. I have accepted it, and even—chosen it. . . . I just want you to keep a tiny place for me in yours. But I was thinking of something, and I meant that I would like to give you more than I do."

The husband of a friend of hers, who had come back from a concentration camp, used to wake up

almost every night screaming: "Don't hit me!"
Kassner had shut his eyes, and Anna thought she
would be afraid when he slept.

"At certain moments," she went on, "I have the
impression that it is not suffering which changes,
but hope. . . ."

Sadly she raised her pale eyes between their long
black lashes and looked up at him with a frown.

Expression by expression, her intelligent face
took on its familiar clarity; it seemed to have re-
gained consciousness; now he knew those few poor
hidden movements which are the secret of a face,
he knew its tears, its love, its sensuality; her features could be for him the features of joy itself.
Whatever humiliation he had known in the prison
cell these eyes could not have known without shar-
ing. As she continued to speak, the lines of suffering
gradually vanished from her face.

"I have invented so many conversations with you
that I'm always afraid of the moment of awakening.
I had promised myself I would not tell you a single

sad thing when the day came. There is more joy in me than . . ."

She could not find the word, and, with a gesture of her hand, recovered her old smile for the first time, which showed her lovely teeth. Finally she said, not without bitterness:

". . . but it does not dare to show itself . . ." as if she were still afraid.

She had not dared to say this until now; was it too soon for even the idea of happiness to rise between them? Life was enveloping him as his arm enveloped her body, was slowly winning him back.

"Perhaps," she said, "I am thinking what to say to you because today I find it hard to think of anything else, but that does not make it wrong. I am not always a very happy woman: I live a difficult life. . . . And yet nothing in the world is more wonderful—nothing—than to know the child is there. And that he is mine. I think of the fact that there are—how many?—five thousand, ten thousand children in this city. And thousands of women who

168

will shortly be seized by labor-pains (they almost always begin around one or two in the morning), and who are waiting. With anguish, yes, but also with something else. Something beside which the word joy has almost no meaning. Nor any other word. And since the world began, every night has been like that."

By her voice he guessed that modesty, and perhaps a remote and superstitious anxiety, made her express her joy in the only images which had remained vivid to her through her months of anguish. They heard the child's voice. But he was not crying, he was talking to himself.

"When he was born, you were in Germany. I awoke, I looked at him, so tiny in his crib, and the thought came to me that his life would be what all life is and I cried my heart out over him and over myself. . . . As I was very weak the tears kept coming and yet from that moment I knew there was something for me which was beyond grief. . . ."

"Men do not have children."

He could not detach his eyes from that face which he had thought dead.

"And yet, in the cells, you see, they need terribly something real, something living, as deeply rooted as pain. . . . Joy has no language."

"For me, joy was music. . . ."

"I have a horror of music now."

She was about to ask why, and instinctively checked herself. He felt that she listened to him more with her body than with her mind, as a mother, and understood far more than his words. The thought shaped itself obscurely in his mind that man had become man in spite of prison cells, in spite of cruelty, and that dignity alone, perhaps, could offset pain. . . . But he felt like looking at Anna, not like thinking. Someone suddenly knocked at a near-by door. Kassner once again heard the knocks of the prison: but she had been more startled than he:

170

"I thought it was you who were coming!"

A door opened amid a hum of cordial voices—an earthly door, human voices. . . .

"I should like to write again," he said. "In the cell I tried to use music to—to defend myself. For hours. It produced images, naturally, an endless stream of them—and, by chance, a sentence, a single sentence, the call of the caravaneers: 'And if this night should be a night of destiny . . .'"

She seized his hand, lifted it to her forehead; and, pressing her face against the back of it, she murmured:

". . . may it be blessed until the coming of dawn . . ."

She had looked away into the night, her profile barely emerging from the hand which she kept in hers. It had been raining, and a car passed over the wet paving with the sound of leaves rustling in the wind. Framed by the window, Anna's eye, half hidden by the hand, seemed to be staring at the corner of the two deserted streets. Kassner knew that as long as he lived the image of that corner house would remain vivid.

In a low voice Anna said:

"Even your going away again shortly—I am ready to . . . better than you think. . . ."

She had wanted to say "accept it." The house had six windows, three on each side—and two dormer windows; they were all in shadow, yet brighter than the sky because of some glimmer caught by the glass still glistening with rain, and the whole night was relaxing as Anna's arms had relaxed a while ago. One of those moments which make men believe a god has just been born flooded the house from which a boy came out only to vanish in the shadow, and it seemed to Kassner that, out of the blood-stained earth, the true meaning of existence was emerging, and that the earth's obscure destiny was about to be realized. He closed his eyes: touch penetrated farther than all the other senses, farther than thought itself, and only the pressure of Anna's brow against his fingers was in harmony with the peace of the earth. He saw himself again running round the cell—one, two, three, four—to find out if she was alive. He opened his eyes again immediately and it seemed to him that he held their eternity in his grasp, an eternity composed of his fellow-prisoners of yesterday, of the child's trusting cheek, of the crowd loyally clinging to its companions in torture, of the face of the pilot in the hurricane, of the man who had given himself up for him, even of his forthcoming return to Germany, the eternity of the living and not the eternity of the dead; it swept everything along with it, and, meeting in the very pulsation of his blood with the only thing in man that was greater than man—the gift of manhood—it beat with great throbs through the once more deserted street where the wind was beginning to rise. The memory of his acts would be like the memory of his comrades' blood, and on the day of his death in Germany this moment would die with him. He suddenly felt that he could not endure to remain motionless:

"I feel like walking, like going out with you—anywhere!"

"I must go and get someone to take care of the baby."

She went out. He turned out the light, let the earthly night enter, looked once more at the two still deserted streets. A cat darted round the corner, on swift mouse-like feet.

They were now going to speak, remember, exchange experiences. . . . All this would become a part of every day life, a stairway which they would descend side by side, into the street, under the sky eternally looking down upon the defeats or victories of men's wills.